DAVENPORT HOUSE 2

HOUSE 2

—— A NEW CHAPTER ——

DAVENPORT HOUSE 2

A NEW CHAPTER

MARIE SILK

ISBN 978-0-9973352-3-1 (print)

ISBN 978-0-9973352-4-8 (ebook)

Marie Silk Publishing
P.O. Box 873
Hayden ID 83835
mariesilkpublishing@gmail.com

Davenport House Books by Marie Silk

CHAPTER 1

"You may choose any room in the house, Clara. This is your home now," Mary Davenport said to her sister after dinner. The two girls took their time wandering through the upstairs bedrooms in the vast Colonial mansion. There were twenty bedrooms upstairs, although only a few of them were furnished as bedrooms while the rest remained empty. Clara decided that she liked one room in particular. From the large windows, she could see the stable in the distance.

"I choose this one," she said confidently.

"You are in luck. It is already furnished," remarked Mary, happy to see her sister getting what she deserved for the first time. The girls had been through so much in the last weeks, that this search for a proper bedroom for Clara felt like a holiday from it all. Clara had worked as a housemaid in Davenport House for many years, but now she was being recognized as the daughter of the late Mr. Davenport. Mary did not seem concerned that her newly discovered sister was an illegitimate child of their shared father. She only wanted for Clara to feel at home in the house and treated as an equal member of the family.

"I will move my things in this instant," Clara said excitedly about the room she chose.

"Tomorrow, we will speak with your mother about hiring more staff. There is only Cecelia cleaning rooms now, and the workload is too much for one maid. You may borrow some of my dresses until we go into town again," said Mary.

"Thank you, Mary," Clara replied. "This day has been a dream come true."

John Smith, who was the groundskeeper for Davenport Estate, was cooking dinner in his modest farmhouse kitchen when his housemate Dr. William Hamilton walked in. It had been a hard day and William looked weary as he slowly lowered himself onto a chair, looking as if every movement pained him.

"How is the Robinson baby?" asked John Smith carefully.

"She will live," replied William in a low voice. "I barely made it in time, John. I must set up a clinic in town. People's lives are at stake."

"I see. Did you inquire at the old mining office? It has been vacant since they built the new one."

"I did inquire, but I cannot afford the payments. I am nearly out of money," explained William, still shaken from the visit at the Robinson house.

"It is no wonder you are out of money. You have not charged a nickel since you came here," said John.

William looked up at him. "I cannot charge these people, John. It is not like Philadelphia where the people who came into the clinic had money to spare. Here in the country…it is much different. The Robinsons could not even pay for the bandages and ointments, let alone a fee for the visit. I do not know how I am going to do this. I would not want to overstay my welcome with you, either."

"You need not worry about that. This is your home until you have your new place. Have you talked to Miss Mary about this? She may be able to—"

"It would not be right of me to ask her for money. She is generous enough that she might give to me whatever I ask without hesitation. I could not take advantage of such a person," William replied.

"You are a good soul, but you will never make the money you need if you do not charge folks for your services," John said honestly.

"When I first came here, I planned to open a clinic which I would also reside in to save expenses. But when I encountered the families in the country with so little means…my conscience has not let me charge them. I ended up paying for most of the medicines and supplies myself. And it is not only a clinic in Yorktown that is needed. It took me three hours to ride to the Robinson house tonight, and I could not help but think that I could have made more visits in less time with a motor car. I have applied for grants, but those take time." William stopped and sighed heavily. "I am at least grateful that the Robinson baby will live today."

John Smith was deep in thought as William spoke. They ate their dinner, and William soon fell asleep in the chair he was seated in.

At Davenport House the next morning, Clara sat at the breakfast table with Mary and Abigail. Abigail was Mary's companion who also lived in the house. Clara was wearing an afternoon dress that she borrowed from Mary that day. Clara was taller than Mary, so the dress was short on her, but Clara did not seem to mind as she enjoyed every delectable bite of breakfast. Clara's aunt Catherine was the cook for Davenport House, and renowned for her delicious cooking.

"Catherine's cooking is fine to be sure, but I do believe she made this meal especially for you, Clara," said Mary with a smile. Clara smiled back. Her aunt was proud of Clara's new position in the house.

"Would you like me to ask Catherine if there is more, Miss Mary?" asked Mrs. Price, who was the housekeeper as well as Clara's mother.

"Oh I have eaten so much that I do not think I can fit another bite. Perhaps if Abigail or Clara would like some more…" Mary trailed off.

"I will have a riding lesson soon, so I should not have any more. Although the food is delicious," said Abigail shyly.

"I might take another plate if I had any room left at all. I think I should wait for lunch," said Clara.

"Very good," said Mrs. Price, and she tidied the dishes on the buffet.

"Let us meet in the upstairs sitting room to discuss the staff, Mrs. Price," ordered Mary.

"Very good, Miss Mary," Mrs. Price replied.

Ethan was waiting at the stable for Abigail to arrive and begin her riding lesson. He saddled a horse named Amethyst, who was an appropriate riding choice for beginners. Abigail nervously approached the stable while wearing Mary's riding clothes. Abigail had worked as a hotel maid before she was hired at Davenport House only weeks ago. She did not own a set of her own riding clothes and often borrowed Mary's. Abigail had only one dress when she first became Mary's companion, and Mary generously purchased some lovely apparel for her recently.

"Good morning, Abigail," greeted Ethan, who managed the horses and stable of Davenport Estate. "Are you feeling good about riding today?"

"I am trying to," she said while forcing a smile. "I did have fun at my last riding lesson."

"We will try to make sure that happens again," Ethan said smiling as he helped her onto the horse.

Back at the house in the upstairs sitting room, Mary, Clara, and Mrs. Price met to speak about the staff. Sunlight flooded in through the large windows causing the room to feel warm and cheery on the cool April day. "Mrs. Price, have you spoken with Clara about what position you wish to take for yourself?" asked Mary.

"I have not thought of it, Miss Mary. It is all so new and sudden that we have not gone that far in the discussion," answered Mrs. Price.

"I understand. I would like to suggest that you find a new housekeeper and take an active role in Clara's finances. I will be transferring to her five hundred acres and she must learn how to manage her property and income from the tenants. As Clara's mother, you are also welcome to take a room in the upstairs as well as dine with us as a member of the family," Mary explained. Clara smiled at her mother.

Mrs. Price looked overwhelmed. "A new housekeeper?" she asked in surprise. It had been her life at Davenport House for over twenty years.

"Yes, I believe that we should face the reality that the

structure of our house and staff will never be the same. I was not even sure whether to keep Cecelia on as a housemaid after the incident with my mother, but she is the only maid that we have right now. We will need at least two more housemaids: one to attend to Clara and me, and the other to fill in where needed. Since you know this house better than anyone Mrs. Price, I will leave the decisions for how to manage this transition in your hands entirely," said Mary.

"Mother, you could have the room next to mine. It is lovely and so much more spacious than your room downstairs," said Clara with a grin.

"Thank you, Child. I must think about how to do this. I have wanted you to have a proper place in this house all your life, but now that the day is here, I am not certain what I should do with myself."

"You may take all the time you need in deciding upon a new housekeeper Mrs. Price, but please find us new maids for the house as quickly as possible," said Mary.

"Very good, Miss Mary," she answered.

"I have wondered if I should take Davenport for my surname now," said Clara proudly.

"I had not thought of that. I am afraid that our family name is tainted with scandal at the moment, with Mother and Richard incarcerated. But I understand of course that you would like to be recognized as our father's daughter. You must do as you see fit," encouraged Mary.

Abigail rode her horse down the trail with Ethan riding alongside her. "You are doing well today," he said to her.

"Thank you," replied Abigail, although she was certain that he was just being kind.

"How are things going at the house?" asked Ethan.

"Better than expected. I believe that Mary is adjusting to her new life and focusing on the good that came out of the unfortunate events."

Ethan nodded. "I am glad she has you."

"Thank you," said Abigail blushing. They returned to the stable and Ethan helped Abigail down from her horse.

"There is something I have been wanting to tell you about," began Ethan.

"Oh?" said Abigail in surprise. "What is it?"

"Son?" interrupted the voice of Ethan's father, John Smith. "Are you out here?"

"I am here, Pa," Ethan called back, looking at Abigail apologetically. John Smith walked into the stable. Even though he was the groundskeeper of the estate, he was hardly seen by the residents or even his son, now that he moved into the farmhouse. It was only the second time that Abigail had seen what Ethan's father looked like since she began employment at the house.

"Good afternoon, Miss," said John Smith when he saw Abigail. "I do not wish to interrupt your lesson. I can return later."

"We have just finished," said Abigail shyly. "I should be getting back to the house."

"Will you be back tomorrow?" Ethan asked her, then he remembered to introduce her. "I am sorry. Pa, this is Abigail. She is Miss Mary's companion."

"Pleased to meet you, Abigail," said John Smith.

"Thank you, I am pleased to meet you properly, Mr. Smith," she replied. The three of them stood there awkwardly.

"Abigail, may I ask a favor of you? Will you tell Miss Mary that I wish to speak with her?" asked John Smith timidly.

"I will be glad to, Mr. Smith," replied Abigail, and she walked back to the house.

John Smith noticed that Ethan was in a daze while watching her walk away. "She seems a nice girl," he said to his son.

Ethan snapped out of it. "Oh, yes, she is nice," he replied distractedly. "Is there something you wished to speak to me about, Pa?"

"There is. I think that I will move into the loft here once more," his father replied. John Smith had lived in the loft above the stable with Ethan for many years until just recently, when the late Master of Davenport House willed a farmhouse to him.

"Is the farmhouse not working out?" asked Ethan in surprise.

"I don't think it is for me anymore," his father answered.

"If you say so, Pa. I will help you move your things whenever you need."

Abigail met Mary and Clara in the upstairs sitting room. Clara was already chatting excitedly about the shopping trip they planned to take in Philadelphia. "Abigail," Mary greeted her. "How was your riding lesson?"

"It was lovely. I was nervous at first, but I think I did better than last time," Abigail replied. "John Smith came into the stable when my lesson was over. He asked me to tell you that he wishes to speak with you, Mary."

"John Smith wishes to speak with me?" Mary repeated in surprise. "I wonder what about. I will go to the stable to see if he is still there." Mary left the room and Abigail and Clara sat in awkward silence.

"How do you like your new room?" asked Abigail kindly.

"I like it very much. I know it is on the opposite side of the house from the rest of the family bedrooms, but it does have a splendid view of the stable," Clara said, then cringed when she realized that she mentioned the stable. She had not intended to say that part out loud.

"I am happy for you," said Abigail. It was silent again for a moment and Abigail wondered if she should say something. "Um, Clara...I hope you don't mind, but I noticed that your dress is a little short. I would be happy to take out the hem for you, if you wish. I do not know if Mary told you, but I used to work as a seamstress."

"It is kind of you to offer. I am afraid that all of Mary's dresses are as short on me as this one. Would you mind terribly letting out more than just the one?" Clara asked.

"I would be glad to. Bring the dresses you wish to have altered to my bedroom. I will have them done very quickly."

Mary went to the stable and found Ethan and John Smith conversing there. "Good afternoon, Miss Mary," Ethan greeted her with a smile. He was glad to see his friend looking well today.

"Good afternoon, Ethan, Mr. Smith," said Mary. "Abigail said you wished to see me?"

"Yes, Miss Mary. It is about the property your father bequeathed to me," he started. "I would like to ask your permission to sell it and move back into the loft here in the stable. I already know of a buyer for the farmhouse."

Mary was surprised. "Oh, I see. The property is yours

to do with as you wish. You need not ask my permission. Is the farmhouse not to your liking?"

"It is, Miss Mary, but it is a big house for only me to live in. I am better suited to the stable here I think."

"However you see fit," assured Mary. She paused for a moment, remembering her friend who also lived in the farmhouse. "Has William found another place to live?"

"William is moving to Yorktown," answered John Smith.

"I see," said Mary, trying to hide her disappointment. "I do wish you luck with your sale."

"Thank you, Miss Mary," said John Smith. He collected a pair of shears and headed for the gardens.

"Do you know what all that was about?" Mary asked Ethan. "Does your pa need the money?"

"If he does, he has not said so to me. Only that he wishes to move into the loft again," replied Ethan. "I expect we will not see William much anymore since he is the only doctor in town now."

"Yes, of course," Mary said. She wanted to see William and talk to him after everything that had happened, but she was not going to say so to Ethan. "Will you please saddle Dolly for me? I will take a short ride before I go back to the house."

Mrs. Price knew a family of little means who lived near Yorktown and had nine daughters. The eldest daughter Fiona sometimes helped Mrs. Price with various errands when the workload at Davenport House became excessive. Mrs. Price wondered if Fiona and one of her sisters might become suitable housemaids with the proper training. She went to call on the Miller family today at their farmhouse.

"Mrs. Price!" Fiona greeted her eagerly at the door

while holding a baby on her hip. She had to speak loudly because inside the house was filled with the noise of babies and small children. "Do you have a job for me? I can help with anything."

"I may have something for you at the house. A permanent position," answered Mrs. Price.

"You could not have come at a better time, Mrs. Price," called Mrs. Miller as she walked outside to greet her, also holding a baby on her hip. "My husband is laid up with sickness and has missed two days' wages."

"Good afternoon, Mrs. Miller. I have been tasked with finding new housemaids for Davenport House. I wondered if Fiona and perhaps another one of your daughters might be suited for the job."

Mrs. Miller raised her eyebrows. "Housemaids? My girls? The wages would be welcome, but I do depend on the girls to help me with the younger ones," Mrs. Miller said wearily. She had birthed two sets of twins within the past three years.

"Of course, Mrs. Miller," replied Mrs. Price. "Please allow me to explain that your daughters, if they prove to be right for the job, would have room and board at Davenport House as well as a starting wage of six dollars per month."

Fiona's face lit up. "Six dollars a month! Mother, isn't it wonderful?"

Mrs. Miller's eyes grew wide. She smiled as she used her available hand to smooth her hair while her other arm held the baby. "How many of my daughters do you need, Mrs. Price?"

Mary rode over to the farmhouse where John Smith and William were living. She noticed that William's horse was there grazing in the pasture, indicating that William must be inside the house. Mary knocked on the door hopefully. There was no answer for a moment and Mary knocked again. When she did not hear an answer still, she walked back to Dolly.

"Mary?" called William's voice from the house. "Is everyone alright?"

Mary turned around. "Good afternoon—we are all well," she stammered.

"I am glad to hear it. Have you come to see John?" William asked, walking outside toward Mary.

"I came to see if you were here, but I thought you must be away when there was no answer," replied Mary.

"Oh I am sorry. I fell asleep and did not hear at first. I have made house calls since dawn," said William, stifling a yawn. "I am glad to see you. Thank you for visiting."

"Oh yes, of course. I am sorry if I woke you though," apologized Mary.

"No need to apologize. It is a pleasant surprise to be woken when no one is ill," laughed William. "I must be up anyway to leave for town again."

"I see. Well I should let you be on your way then," said Mary.

"I can stay a moment for you, Mary. Was there something you wished to see me about?" asked William.

Mary felt awkward. She was not sure if this was the time to explain about all that had happened since she saw him last. She worried that he might see her as a nuisance while he had more important things to do. She decided to take the conversation a different direction. "When should we expect a bill for your services this past week?"

"Oh," William said uncomfortably. "I had not planned on charging you. You are my friends and it was my pleasure to help."

Mary smiled. She was at least glad to hear him call her a friend. "It is generous of you William, but it is only right that we pay you. Dr. Jones used to be a family friend, yet he still charged us plenty and often, I assure you."

William smiled. "Mary, I have a confession to make. I am no businessman. I chose medicine for a career because I wished to help people who needed it. My schooling never included how to charge my friends or people who did not have the means to pay."

"I have the means to pay, so you need not worry about sending us a bill," Mary told him.

"Thank you, Mary," said William sheepishly. They stood silently for a moment. Mary wondered why he did not tell her that he was moving into Yorktown, or anything else at all.

"I should be getting to town now," said William. "As always, tell me if there is anything that you may need."

"Just the bill please, Dr. Hamilton," said Mary smiling, and she walked back to Dolly to ride home.

CHAPTER 2

Mrs. Price began training the two new house-maids, Fiona and Bridget Miller. They were young girls but already knew the meaning of hard work from their busy home life. Their eagerness to learn and do well was the quality that Mrs. Price was looking for. Cecilia, the housemaid who had worked at Davenport House for the last five years, was a rather silly girl. She got the job done, but always seemed to have a crisis while doing so. It was especially true lately during all of the changes to the house. Mrs. Price was relieved to be working with two girls of sense now.

"Fiona, once you learn your duties, you will be attending to Miss Mary and Miss Clara. Bridget will fill in when needed but will clean the house with Cecilia for most of the day," explained Mrs. Price.

"Yes, Mrs. Price," the girls said in unison.

Abigail knocked on Clara's new bedroom door before breakfast. "Come in," answered Clara. She was sprawled out on the elegant bed, enjoying the feel of the plush mattress and smooth quilt made of silk. "Why is it so difficult to leave these marvelous beds in the morning?"

Abigail giggled as she entered with two of Clara's dresses draped over her arm. "Because sleeping on these beds is like sleeping on a cloud. I am still getting used to it myself."

Clara smiled and sat up. "Oh, you have finished the dresses. Thank you."

"It was my pleasure," said Abigail as she hung the dresses in the wardrobe. "These new lengths should work nicely on you."

"How do you like my new room?" beamed Clara.

"It is lovely," said Abigail while looking around. "What a difference it is from the servants' quarters. There is so much color and light in these rooms."

Clara got out of bed and went to the window. "The window in my other room was scarcely the size of a book. This one takes up almost the entire wall. I do like looking out of it every day to see the outside."

"I am happy for you, Clara," said Abigail kindly. "Now that you have proper dresses to wear, I will see you downstairs at breakfast."

William awoke to the sound of items clattering together. He had fallen asleep in the kitchen chair again, and John was making a racket of something in the next room.

"I'm awake now!" William shouted with a laugh as he got up to find John. "Are you alright in there?"

"Just fine," answered John.

"Are you...packing for a trip?"

"I am moving back into the stable loft with my boy."

"Oh," said William in surprise. "Today?"

"I sold the house. New buyer wants to move in tomorrow," replied John.

"I see. I will get my things together also," William said uncertainly.

"Wait," said John reaching into his pocket to pull out an envelope. "This is for you."

William took the envelope. It was full of money. "John, how—"

"It's enough to get your clinic set up in town. Enough for a motor car too, and a little more besides," explained John.

William was speechless. Was he to believe that John had sold the only asset he ever owned to give the money up for William's practice? When William finally found his voice, he said seriously, "John. I can't—"

"You must," interrupted John with a shaking voice. "Not for me. For Maryanne. She might still be here if only the doctor had come—" his voice cracked and he turned his face away.

William swallowed the lump in his throat. "I will do as you say, John. For your wife. Thank you."

At Davenport House, the girls were having lunch in the dining room. "Mrs. Price has hired two new housemaids. Have you seen them yet?" Mary asked Abigail and Clara.

"I have seen them," answered Abigail. "I think that they are sisters. The younger one can scarcely be older than fourteen. They do seem happy to have employment here." Abigail looked up from her plate to see Mary smile at Clara, then Clara smile back at Mary. "What is it?" asked Abigail curiously.

"Oh, I forgot to mention. Clara and I will go into town during your riding lesson today," said Mary casually.

"Yes, we will," said Clara smiling. Abigail tried to not feel left out of the girls' trip into town. She knew that things were going to be different between her and Mary now that Mary had a sister to accompany her wherever she went.

Abigail finished her lunch, then went to her room to change into Mary's riding clothes. While she was on her way to the stable, she could see Clara and Mary riding away in the carriage. Ethan was waiting for Abigail with Amethyst and another horse he saddled for himself.

"Good afternoon, Abigail," greeted Ethan when he saw her.

Abigail smiled shyly. She would sometimes forget how handsome Ethan was until she saw him again, then become so shy that she could barely speak. He seemed happy to see her.

"Should we take the easy trail again today?" he asked.

"I think I am ready to try something more challenging," she answered bravely.

Ethan grinned. "I know of a great ride we can take. We will have to leave right away, though. I promised my pa that I would help him move back into the loft tonight."

"He will not live in the farmhouse anymore?" asked Abigail.

"He has sold it. The buyer is set to move in tomorrow so we need to finish with the move tonight."

"I see. Well, let us get started with our ride now so you may be back in time," said Abigail with a smile. They both rode off down a picturesque trail through the woods.

Mary and Clara arrived at Yorktown in the carriage.

They were just heading into a secondhand shop when Mary thought she saw William walking out of the old mining office across the street. "You go on without me, Clara. I will be just a moment," she said, then walked over to the mining office. "William, it *is* you. Good afternoon."

"Mary! Good afternoon," he greeted with a smile. "Can you believe it? I now have a clinic in town! Well, it is not a clinic just yet, but with a little work it will be ready in no time. Come inside and I will show you."

"How wonderful," said Mary. "I would like to see, but I am shopping now with Clara and should not abandon her. May we see it later?'

"Of course," answered William. "I have more good news to tell you then. I will be here the rest of the day, so come in whenever you can."

Mary went into the secondhand shop and saw Clara looking at the jewelry there. "I found it," she told Mary.

"Perfect," said Mary. She talked to the clerk and made her purchase. After placing their things into the carriage with the driver, Mary and Clara walked to the mining office to see William.

"Come in," he welcomed them happily. "The place is a little dusty, but it will be a working clinic by the end of the week!" Mary and Clara walked into the office, the heels of their boots causing echos to travel across the empty room. It was an expansive room with a spiral staircase in the back corner which led to an apartment on the second floor. "Try to imagine a few chairs here, and some beds here with roll-away dividers, and a sign on the door that says 'The Doctor Is In'." William chatted excitedly to the girls about his plans for the clinic. "Best of all, I will be in the town center so it will not take me so long to make house calls. And that is the other good news! I will be going into Philadelphia to purchase a motor car for myself. I can make house calls in the afternoon, then be back by supper time to sleep in the apartment upstairs."

Mary felt joy in watching William's face light up with excitement. "It is brilliant. I congratulate you on your new clinic, Dr. Hamilton," she giggled.

"Yes, congratulations, Dr. Hamilton," repeated Clara awkwardly, hoping that she did not look as out of place as she felt.

Mary then realized that she had forgotten to explain to William about Clara. "We have some good news as well. I have much to tell you when we have more time, but for now, please allow me to introduce my sister, Clara. You have seen her before at the house but she was not given a proper introduction."

William raised his eyebrows. "Your sister? Well, I am pleased to meet you properly this time, Clara."

Clara smiled. "I am pleased to make your acquaintance, Dr. Hamilton." The girls went home in the carriage feeling happier than they had for a long time.

After Abigail's riding lesson, Ethan took a horse-drawn wagon to the farmhouse to help his father. John Smith did not have very many things to move, so it did not take long to load the wagon. He saved one particular item to be the very last that they loaded. "Be careful with this one, Son," he said to Ethan. It was a heavy wooden chest with ornate carvings in the top and sides. It looked rather out of place alongside John Smith's plain belongings.

"I have not seen this before. Was this my mother's?"

Ethan asked, although he could not think of any other reason his father might have it.

His father nodded. "She called it her 'hope chest'," he answered sadly. "Now it holds everything that she left behind." John Smith usually kept the chest covered with a quilt so that it would not get damaged.

"I will be careful with it, Pa." They gently loaded the hope chest into the wagon and made their way to the stable.

Abigail knocked on Mary's bedroom door. "Come in," said Mary. "Oh you have brought the riding clothes with you. How was your lesson?"

"It was splendid. I believe I will be ready to ride alongside you the next time, Mary," said Abigail confidently.

"Wonderful! Ethan is a fine instructor. Oh, that reminds me—Nellie will be coming to visit us on Thursday. I wonder if it will be quite as wild as the last time she came," Mary said as they laughed together. "I must tell her all of our news. She will be so surprised about Clara being my sister! I am glad that Nellie will not shun us like the other families have. She is too rich to care what others think."

Clara was in her bedroom admiring her new dress from Yorktown. Fiona was attending to her tonight, and Clara patiently explained to her the role of an attending maid. Fiona stumbled a bit at first, but was determined to do the job correctly. "How old are you?" Clara asked her.

"Sixteen, Miss Clara," answered Fiona. Clara smiled. She never thought a servant would address her as 'Miss' anything in her whole life.

"I am almost ashamed to say how old I am, since I have never married. Many girls are married at eighteen now, and I am twenty-five. Some would call me an old maid. I have been engaged before, but it was not meant to be. I would like to get married by the end of the year if only I can find the right man…" Clara rambled. She was so used to feeling invisible as a maid that it was a relief to be able to speak her mind to someone who was listening. Clara wore her new dress to dinner and the other girls remarked on how beautiful she looked. Clara found herself basking in this new feeling of importance.

CHAPTER 3

It was the twenty-first of April in 1915. Abigail sat in front of her vanity table looking into the mirror. She usually wore her long hair down over her shoulders, but today she took her hair in her hands and carefully styled the dark curls up above her neck, holding them in place with bobby pins. Bobby pins were now being sold in every town to hold the new bob haircuts that other girls began wearing. Abigail hoped that her hair looked properly styled today. She took a deep breath and went down to breakfast.

Mary and Clara were already enjoying crepes with raspberry jam at the dining table. They seemed to be smiling knowingly at each other and giggling throughout the meal. Abigail suspected there must be a secret between them. She hoped that her new hairstyle did not make her look too silly to them.

"I think that we should take a welcome basket to our new neighbors tomorrow," said Mary. "John Smith has told me that the new residents of the farmhouse are a family with small children. They are the only neighbors we will have within walking distance, so we may as well get to know them."

"A very good idea, Mary. It will be a fun surprise for them," Clara said with a twinkle in her eye.

"Let us go to the drawing room, now that we are finished," ordered Mary with a smile. Abigail followed the girls into the drawing room. It looked nothing like it had in the past with only plain furnishings and a fireplace. Today it was decorated with flowers and balloons, and a large banner that hung from the ceiling:

HAPPY BIRTHDAY ABIGAIL

Abigail gasped in disbelief. "This is for me? How did you know?"

Mary and Clara were giggling again. "Mrs. Price told us, and we have been forced to keep the secret for days!" said Mary.

"Oh, it is beautiful. What a surprise! I have never had a birthday celebration before. This is too much," Abigail said with tears in her eyes. She had to sit down on the chair.

"There is more to the surprise," said Clara cheerfully. "This is from me." She handed Abigail a gift wrapped in brown paper and ribbon. Abigail opened the paper carefully to reveal a delightful white blouse and long blue skirt.

"How marvelous," said Abigail. "Now I see why you took the carriage into town so mysteriously the other day. Thank you, dear Clara."

"I have something for you as well," Mary said, giving Abigail a rectangle-shaped box wrapped with pink ribbon. Abigail opened the box and gasped at the costly pearl necklace that lay within it.

"Your hair does look lovely today, Abigail," remarked Mary. "I am glad that we could surprise you."

"Thank you Mary," said Abigail, blushing as Mary put the necklace on her.

The housemaids were having their early lunch in the kitchen. Fiona and Bridget were glad to eat three times a day while they worked at Davenport House. At their family's home, they were fortunate to eat twice a day. "Cecelia, why do Miss Mary and Miss Clara have a maid to attend them, but not Miss Abigail?" asked Bridget curiously.

Cecelia was a maid who had worked at Davenport House since she was nineteen. She was a short girl with a thick waist and had a habit of scurrying about the house to eavesdrop on the family rather than getting her work done. She knew more about the recent family scandal than the other servants did. She seemed excessively gratified now that the new maid asked her this question. "Well, it is because Abigail is not even part of the family! She used to be a maid here. And before that, she used to work at a hotel!" Cecelia answered dramatically. "I would never wait on her."

Mrs. Price overheard the maids' conversation. "Cecelia! You will never wait on anyone in the family if I hear such talk from you again," she said sternly.

"Yes, Mrs. Price," Cecelia hung her head.

"Bridget, in answer to your question, Abigail is a lady's companion to Miss Mary. Abigail may employ her own maid if she wishes but she prefers not to. Miss Mary and Miss Clara are Davenports, and Davenports have attending maids," Mrs. Price explained.

Bridget and Fiona nodded in response. "Have their parents

died?" asked Fiona. Cecelia perked up at another chance to gossip. One look from Mrs. Price changed her mind.

"All you need to know for now is that Miss Mary and Miss Clara are in charge," said Mrs. Price.

William was busy setting up his new clinic in Yorktown. The money that he received from John enabled him to order several hospital beds with room dividers and other supplies for the clinic. Just now, there were only a desk and three chairs in the clinic. It was the closest thing to a hospital that the growing city of Yorktown would have available. William watched his money carefully so that he could purchase a motor car the following week. He also watched the newspapers daily, as tensions from the Great War in Europe along with anti-German sentiments in America were increasing. He was reading the newspaper that day when there was a knock on the door of the clinic.

"Mary," William smiled as he opened the door.

"Before you ask—" she began with a smile. "—we are all well. I wanted to see you. I hope you remember that I am your friend and do not only wish to see you when one of us is ill," she said honestly.

"I have not forgotten, Mary. I wish I could see you more often," William replied just as honestly. He pulled out a chair for her and sat down across from her.

Mary's heart beat faster as she sat down. "You do?" she asked anxiously. She was worried that he might not want to see her every day as much as she longed to see him.

"Of course I do," he looked into her eyes and spoke sincerely. He did not know what to say next, so they sat there in silence.

"Is there anything I may do to help with the clinic?"

Mary finally asked. "Do you have enough funds for your medical equipment?"

"I do have the funds now. John has been very generous to me," William said quietly.

"John Smith?" Mary asked surprised. "Oh! Is this what the sale of the farmhouse was about?"

William nodded. "He knew that I could not have paid for it on my own. I was stunned when John gave me the funds to make all of this possible, and I felt undeserving for not having earned it myself. I know that he loves his wife very much to this day. She was a great lady and very beautiful. I was only a boy when I met her. I remember her being so kind to me." William noticed tears forming in Mary's eyes when he mentioned John's wife. "Did you know her—before?"

"She was my nurse at the house," Mary whispered. "She raised me."

"Oh...I did not realize. Then, you know how she was. A few nights ago, I came home from a house call where the child nearly died because it took me so long to get there. I was broken up about it when I got back to the farmhouse. I talked to John that night, and the next thing I knew, he sold his house and gave the money to me. At first I could not think of taking his money, but he insisted that I do so in her memory," William explained as a tear fell down his cheek. "He knew I could not refuse when he spoke her name."

"I understand now," said Mary quietly.

"Thank you for visiting me today, Mary. It is wonderful to have someone to talk to who understands."

Mary nodded. "If there is anything I may do to help, you need only ask."

"There is something I must ask of you," he replied seriously. "The War is only getting worse. I am afraid that Americans may have to join the fight at any moment. Unfortunately for my family and me, there is growing animosity toward Germans. I have decided that I will conceal my German roots from my clients and the rest of the town to keep the peace within the clinic. You, John, and Abigail are the only ones who know."

Mary smiled and looked in his eyes. "We will not speak of it to anyone. I promise."

Abigail retired to her bedroom after dinner. She enjoyed a wonderful birthday with the celebration and gifts from Mary and Clara. She was just about to change into her nightclothes when there was a knock at the door.

"Good evening, Fiona," Abigail greeted when she opened the door.

"Good evening, Miss Abigail. I have finished my duties for the night and came to see if there was anything you needed before I went back downstairs."

"Oh, you are very kind to ask. I do not need anything. I was just about to go to sleep for the night," she answered.

"Very good, Miss," Fiona said, and she left for the servants' stairs.

Abigail smiled and closed her door. She started to reach into her hair to begin removing bobby pins when she heard a light tapping sound, like something fell against the bedroom window. Then she heard it again. She held her breath to listen if it would happen again, and it did. She went over to the window and moved the curtain to the side. She giggled when she realized what the sound was. Ethan was standing below the window and throwing small twigs at it. He waved and smiled when she looked out the window. Abigail put her sweater on then quietly went downstairs and through the front door. She giggled again as she walked across the cold grass to where Ethan stood. "What is this all about? Did you intend to get my window?"

Ethan laughed. "Of course I knew it was yours. This was how I used to get Miss Mary to come out and play when we were young, and then you told me that you have her old room. I thought you might ride Amethyst today, but when I did not see you at the stable, I knew I must come speak with you before you went to sleep."

"It sounds urgent," remarked Abigail playfully. "What is it?"

Ethan held out an object in his hand. Abigail tried to see what it was in the dark, but her eyes had not adjusted. "It is for you," said Ethan. "For your birthday."

Abigail was glad that he could not see her blushing in the dark. "Thank you," she said as she took it from his hand. It was a wood carving of a horse. "Oh, it is brilliant. Is this a hobby of yours?"

"Only for special occasions," he replied. "Have you done something different with your hair today?"

"I am eighteen now. I will wear it up like this from now on," she explained shyly.

"Oh, I see. You—you have done a nice job putting it up like that," he stammered.

"Thank you," she whispered.

"Happy Birthday, and goodnight, Abigail."

"Goodnight."

CHAPTER 4

Nellie Whitmore's eyes grew wide as Mary revealed the truth about Clara being a Davenport in painstaking detail. Nellie loved a good story. She was having tea with Mary, Clara, and Abigail in the upstairs sitting room that afternoon. "Well! Who would have guessed it? You two don't look a thing alike," Nellie commented while looking back and forth between them. Then she laughed. "You are lucky. My family does not have any interesting secrets at all!"

The girls laughed with her. It was a relief to be able to speak the truth of their circumstances without the worry of facing judgment. "Oh, poor Clara, you have had no proper debutante. I will make introductions for you. You must learn how to navigate society and you must do it quickly," said Nellie with a twinkle in her eye.

Clara was elated. "Would you truly introduce me?"

"Of course! It would be such fun! Oh dear, it may have to wait though. I have nearly forgotten that I am sailing for Liverpool in just over a week! I must think up a plan. In the meantime, let us take a walk to the stable—to see the horses of course."

John Smith was living with Ethan in the stable loft once more. He went back to the farmhouse to help the new owner settle in. The father was a widower called Phillip Valenti with a young boy and girl to raise by himself. He had the same lost look that John remembered having himself when he was left to raise a child in the midst of grief. Phillip Valenti had escaped the hustle and bustle of Pittsburgh in favor of a quiet country life and living off the land.

"Thank you for helping us get in so quickly, John," said Phillip. "It is not so simple with the little ones."

John nodded. "We are just a walk to the north if you find yourself needing anything."

Ethan became nervous when he saw Nellie Whitmore, Mary, Clara, and Abigail walking in his direction. "This is going to be interesting," he muttered to himself. The four girls looked like proper ladies. Each wore her hair styled up perfectly, and dressed in a cheerful pastel skirt with white blouse, except for Mary who was still wearing her black mourning attire. "Good afternoon, Ladies," Ethan greeted. "Will you be wanting to ride today?"

"Oh, we are just taking a walk. Won't you come with us?" coaxed Nellie. In the past, Nellie had told Mary that Ethan was the handsomest man she had ever known. She liked to see him every time she visited Davenport House. "It seems so long since I saw you last, Ethan. How have you been?"

"Fine thank you, Miss Whitmore," he replied as he

joined the girls. They walked the perimeter around the fence and watched the horses graze in the pasture.

"My stable is nearly empty now," remarked Nellie. "I have not used the carriage at all since buying the automobile. All that remain are horses for the servants and a riding horse for me. I think the stable boys are worried they may be out of a job soon."

"I have considered an automobile for the house, but I have been busy of course with managing the estate. We could not live without Ethan though," Mary said as she looked back and smiled at him. "William said that he will buy an automobile next week for his medical practice."

"Oh yes, your new doctor. Have you fainted again while he is nearby, Mary?" Nellie teased. Mary turned red and looked away.

"I did enjoy the car ride to Philadelphia with you, Nellie," said Abigail, trying to save Mary from further embarrassing questions. "But I have become quite taken with horseback riding now."

"I am glad to hear it. And what do you think about it Clara?" asked Nellie, making sure to include her new friend in the conversation. "Do you prefer to ride horseback as well?"

"I have never learned to ride," admitted Clara. "I have only gone by carriage in the past, but I would like to live as modern as possible now. If I have the chance to ride in an automobile sometime, I believe I might never think of a horse again."

"There is much to see, Clara. I cannot wait to show you. Oh, I have just realized a perfect solution! You must come to New York and take the voyage to Liverpool with me! I will introduce you to London society, who will not have heard a thing about your past. You may even fall in love with a man of title there. They are wild about rich American girls. I can hardly keep them away. It is a splendid idea, you must come," Nellie chatted excitedly.

Clara was beaming. She had been wanting the chance to see the world away from Davenport House for years. Ethan watched Clara's reaction, and Abigail watched them both. Abigail had been under the impression that Clara and Ethan were engaged in secret.

"What a grand opportunity for you leave and meet new people, Clara," remarked Mary in awe. "What do you think?"

"Nothing would make me happier!" Clara exclaimed. "But, did you not say that you are leaving next week? Do we have enough time to arrange it?"

"Oh, I will handle that, don't you worry. I will just telephone them to change my reservation. Honestly Mary, you are living in the Dark Ages out here with no automobile or telephone. Clara, you will love the Lusitania. It is gorgeous! The dining room is like a palace," Nellie continued on about the beautiful ship.

Clara could hardly contain her excitement. "I will need new dresses! Oh, I cannot believe it!"

"We will arrive in New York a day early so we can buy whatever you need there. If you like modern, you will fall in love with New York," said Nellie.

"I cannot wait," grinned Clara, her heart nearly beating out of her chest.

Clara, Nellie, and Mary walked ahead and discussed their new plan excitedly. Abigail stayed behind a little ways to speak with Ethan. He was quiet and thoughtful.

"Thank you for the birthday gift," Abigail said to him. "I was impressed when I could see it in the light. Your carving is very detailed."

"It is supposed to be Amethyst," Ethan replied quietly. "She misses you, you know."

Abigail giggled. "Can horses truly miss people?"

"Of course they can. I see it when they do," replied Ethan seriously. "They have feelings just like us. I have never seen Amethyst miss someone quite so much. She becomes happy whenever you come to ride."

"I cannot tell if you are only teasing me," Abigail said. "Either way, you may tell Amethyst that I will return for a ride after dinner."

Nellie Whitmore left the house shortly after having dinner with the girls. Mary retired to bed, Abigail prepared for her evening ride, and Clara went down to the servants' quarters to find her mother.

"Mother!" Clara exclaimed as she entered her mother's bedroom. "You will never guess what has happened! I have the most exciting news. Miss Nellie Whitmore has invited *me* on a voyage to Great Britain!"

Mrs. Price was aghast. "It cannot be. You must tell her no."

"Why must I tell her no?" Clara demanded. "Do you not want me to be happy?"

"Of course I want you to be happy, Child, but it does not seem safe. Have you forgotten the grand ship that went down just years ago? It was all anyone could talk about for the longest time. More than a thousand lives were lost in the water!"

"Mother! It is unlucky to speak of such things when I

am about to embark on a voyage! You are just afraid of me discovering that there is a world outside of this stuffy house."

"But you live upstairs now. You have everything you could ever want, and never need to work again. Please listen to me Clara. I have a terrible feeling about this. Please, tell Miss Whitmore you must abandon this plan," begged Mrs. Price.

"I will do nothing of the kind! I have been given the opportunity of a lifetime by Miss Nellie Whitmore, who knows everyone and everything in London. I am a Davenport now and I must start acting like one. I *will* go on this voyage and I will leave for New York a week from Friday."

Abigail and Ethan rode their horses down a short trail not far from the stable. The half-moon seemed bright that night as they talked about the adventure of night riding. "I admit, it is a thrilling sensation to ride in the dark. I think I see now why Mary enjoys it so much," said Abigail.

"It is adventurous. I often ride out here after everyone has gone to bed. It is a good time to be away from it all and think," Ethan said. "What Miss Whitmore said today about her stable boys being out of work…it made me worry that it might be me someday."

"You must enjoy your work with the horses very much," said Abigail kindly.

"It is all I want to do, but William says the world is changing fast. What if everyone makes the transition to motor cars? Caring for horses is my life."

"You do remember Mary saying that she could not do without you," said Abigail kindly. "Perhaps you never need worry about it."

"We should be getting back now," said Ethan quietly.

"The horses are still in the pasture and I must bring them in for the night."

Clara angrily stormed to her room as she replayed her mother's reaction to her news over and over in her mind. The offer to take a voyage with Nellie was Clara's dream come true, yet her mother spoke as if Clara should actually consider not going. She looked out of her bedroom window toward the stable. She knew that Abigail had gone for an evening ride after dinner. Clara wondered when she and Ethan would be back.

Phillip Valenti went to check on his sleeping children in one of the bedrooms of the farmhouse. Donnie, his three-year-old little boy, was sleeping soundly in the bed. But Gabriella was not in the bed with him. Phillip tried not to panic as he searched the house for his four-year-old daughter. Gabriella was nowhere to be seen.

John Smith was about to retire to bed in the stable loft. He could hear a peculiar noise that sounded like the latch of a stall door clicking against something. He knew that none of the horses were inside, so he took his oil lantern to investigate what caused the sound.

Clara watched from her window as Abigail and Ethan rode toward the stable. She tried to repress the feelings of jealousy that came over her whenever she saw them together. It was not so long ago that Clara and Ethan were planning to marry and move away from Davenport House. Clara sighed heavily as she tried to turn her mind to thoughts of being in London with Nellie Whitmore, surrounded by dozens of noble bachelors.

John Smith walked slowly toward the horse stalls with his lantern in hand. He could see one stall door opening a little ways, then closing repeatedly, but there was no one in sight. He figured it could not be the wind. He bent down to look under the stall door. The door suddenly swung open in front of him, causing John to trip backward and fall to the ground. The lantern slipped from his grasp and was flung onto the dry straw a few feet away, shattering the glass and setting the floor ablaze. In the stall before him stood Phillip Valenti's little girl.

"Do you need any help bringing the horses in?" Abigail asked Ethan when they were nearly to the pasture. Ethan did not answer. He was looking straight ahead and thought he could see an orange glow emanating from inside the stable. He jumped off his horse quickly.

"Pa!" Ethan shouted as he began to run toward the stable. Abigail quickly dismounted and secured the horses within the pasture fence. She could feel her heart pounding in fear.

As Clara looked toward the stable, she noticed that it appeared unnaturally bright. Then she realized what was happening. She ran out of her bedroom to the upstairs hallway, yelling to anyone who could hear, "Fire! The stable is on fire! Help!"

John Smith came running out of the stable toward Ethan and Abigail. He was carrying a little girl that neither of them had ever seen before. He went straight to Abigail and pushed the child into her arms. Then he ran back into the stable.

"Pa, no! The horses are all outside!" Ethan shouted after him. "The stalls are empty! Pa!" When he could see that his father was not returning, Ethan ran after him. Abigail hurried away from the stable with the little girl whose arms clung tightly around her shoulders. Abigail looked behind her in horror as Ethan disappeared into the fiery stable.

"Pa, the horses are out, we have to go!" shouted Ethan through the flames. Then he could see his father in the loft, struggling to carry Maryanne's hope chest down the ladder by himself.

"I can't leave it! I can't lose her again!" his father cried back. Ethan hurried up the ladder and took the other end of the chest. They quickly carried it out of the stable to safety.

Clara, Mary, and the servants stood outside of Davenport House, watching the stable burn brightly in the night. There was nothing that any of them could do about it.

"It is alright Darling, you are alright," said Abigail gently, trying to calm the crying child in her arms. She heaved a sigh of relief when she saw Ethan and his father emerge from the flames in the distance. Then a man that Abigail had never seen before came running toward her.

"Gabriella!" he cried.

"Papa!" Gabriella cried, loosening her hold on Abigail and running to jump into the man's arms. Abigail stood there quietly.

"Oh, thank goodness," he cried as he held his daughter. "Thank you for saving her, Miss. I have been searching for her all night!"

"I am glad she is back with you, Sir," Abigail replied. "But it was not I who saved her. John Smith carried her from the stable when it began to catch fire."

The man looked aghast. "My little girl was in that barn? Oh, dear God!"

"It is alright, Sir," said Abigail gently, now trying to

calm the man. "The people and horses have escaped with their lives."

"I must talk to John. I will go find him. Thank you again Miss—?"

"I am Abigail," she told him.

"And I am Phillip Valenti. Thank you Miss Abigail. Gabriella, tell the lady 'thank you'."

"Thank you Miss Abigail," repeated Gabriella. Phillip carried his daughter while he hurried to find John Smith.

Abigail went to Ethan, who was standing a safe distance from the fire now, watching his home slowly burn to the ground. "I am sorry—" she started to say to him. He suddenly put his arms around her and held her tight.

"I thought my Pa was going to—" his voice cracked and tears fell from his eyes. Abigail hugged him back. In this moment of crisis, neither of them cared who might be watching.

"I hope my Gabriella is not the reason for this fire," Phillip said anxiously to John Smith.

"I am afraid it is all my fault," replied John. "I was startled when I saw the child, and then I dropped my lantern."

"Oh no," Phillip shook his head. "So I do share the blame in this. I went to check on the children, but Gabriella was gone. I should have kept closer watch. I am so sorry, John. Is there anything I can do?"

"We need a place for the horses tonight," said John. "Can we use your barn?"

"Oh yes, of course. I will put Gabriella back to bed, and once she is asleep I will come out to help you."

"Ethan," whispered Abigail while they still stood

embracing. "I think that Mary and the others must be worried sick. I should go to tell them that everyone is safe."

"Yes," he replied as he slowly returned his arms to his sides. "I must talk to Pa about what we will do with the horses tonight."

Mary, Clara, Mrs. Price, and the other servants were relieved when Abigail came running toward them. "Everyone is safe!" she cried. "No one is injured! The horses are alright!"

"Oh thank goodness!" exclaimed Mary with tears in her eyes. "I was so afraid for Ethan and his father! And my dear horses! How did the fire start?"

"We do not yet know how it happened," Abigail answered breathlessly.

"Oh dear. I do not know what we will do with the horses, but I am glad they are alright," said Mary.

Mrs. Price discreetly turned to her daughter. "It is an omen, Clara. You must stay at Davenport House." Clara did not answer. She continued to watch the fire smolder in the distance. Much to everyone's relief, the surrounding land was damp from the recent rain and the fire stayed contained to the stable.

"Miss Mary!" called Ethan as he ran toward them.

Mary went to him and threw her arms around his neck. "I was so worried for you," she cried softly.

"I am well, Miss Mary," said Ethan as he hugged her back. "We will take the horses to the Valentis' barn tonight. Then we must decide where we will board them."

"What caused the fire? And who are the Valentis?" asked Mary.

"Pa said the fire was his fault. He is afraid to speak to

you now," replied Ethan. "The Valentis bought the farm-house. They are the new neighbors."

"Oh, I see. When the horses are secure for the night, you and your pa must come to the house. Mrs. Price will prepare rooms for you."

"Thank you, Miss Mary. I need to get back to the horses now," Ethan said, then he ran back toward the pasture.

"Miss Mary," said Mrs. Price as everyone walked back into the house. "I should inform you that the servants' bed-rooms are full."

"It is alright, Mrs. Price. Please prepare rooms upstairs for Ethan and his father."

"Very good, Miss Mary," replied Mrs. Price.

Abigail offered to stay awake in the Hall to keep watch for Ethan and John Smith. They came to the house well after midnight, carrying a heavy wooden chest between the two of them. Ethan and his father were still covered in soot and followed Abigail wearily as she led them up the grand staircase. Abigail said goodnight and finally retired to bed herself. She fell asleep that night holding a small wooden carving of a horse.

CHAPTER 5

"Please post this immediately, Mrs. Price," said Mary the next day before breakfast. She had written to the horse breeder in Yorktown to ask if the horses of Davenport House might board at the ranch until a new stable could be built. Only Mary and Clara attended breakfast that morning. Abigail was still asleep.

"What will you do about the stable?" Clara asked Mary.

"I must hire some men to build a new one," Mary replied. "We cannot go on without a stable."

"Will Ethan live here in the house with us now?" asked Clara.

Mary laughed. "If I know Ethan, I would say that he probably does not enjoy it here as much as we do. He does not care for fancy things and will likely be anxious to return to a stable loft as soon as one is built. I will invite him to meals in the dining room at least. He will not refuse the food from Catherine once he tries it."

It had just passed lunch time when Abigail awoke for the day. She got dressed and styled her hair up, then went down the hallway to the door of the room she led Ethan to the previous night. She was just about to knock on his door when Bridget called to her from further down the hallway.

"There is no one in the room, Miss Abigail. I just went in to make the bed, but Cecelia must have gotten to it before me," Bridget explained.

"Oh, thank you Bridget," Abigail replied. She went back to her room to gather the clothing she had spent the previous night altering. When she returned to Ethan's room, she slowly opened the door and could see the neatly made bed and a wardrobe on the other side of the room. Abigail draped the clothing over her arms and walked toward the wardrobe to hang it up. When she turned the corner around the bed, she suddenly tripped and crashed to the floor, dropping everything she carried. She looked behind her to see what had caused her to lose her footing.

"Ethan!" she cried. "I am so sorry! I did not see any-one in here!" Abigail was aghast to discover that he had been sleeping on the floor near the side of the bed that was not visible from the doorway. His shirt was rolled up under his head for a pillow. He was startled awake by the crash. Abigail tried to get up quickly so she could run out of the room, but was so nervous and clumsy that she fell back down.

"Wait, Abigail," Ethan said as he sleepily pulled his shirt over his head. "Are you hurt?"

"I am alright, I think. I am desperately sorry! I have not hurt you, have I?" she asked worriedly, covering her red face with her hands.

"You just surprised me," replied Ethan, beginning to laugh. "What are you doing in here?"

"Last night I altered these shirts for you that used to

belong to the Master. Mary was going to give them away, but since I thought you must have lost clothes in that dreadful fire, I was going to put these in the wardrobe for you. The maid told me that your room was empty and I did not see you! I am sorry." Abigail was so embarrassed that tears fell down her cheeks as she spoke.

"You stayed awake last night fixing these up for me? That was kind of you Abigail," Ethan said gently. "It is not your fault that you did not see me. I was afraid that I would get black soot on that fancy quilt so I slept down here instead. Please do not worry. I will put the clothes away myself."

Abigail nodded and Ethan helped her up from the floor. She went back to her room to dry her face and try to calm down.

"Has John Smith left his room yet?" Mary asked Mrs. Price.

"He has, Miss Mary. I believe he has been tending to the gardens all morning."

"Oh, I see. I want to be sure that he knows he is invited to dine with us while he stays in the house. I will go find him," Mary said, and she went out into the gardens. John Smith was pulling weeds from a flower bed when Mary walked up to him.

He stood up and removed his hat when he saw her approach. "Miss Mary, it was all my fault," he said hanging his head. "Please withhold my wages until it covers the damages. I don't deserve special treatment with the fancy room neither."

"Can you tell me what happened last night?" asked Mary curiously. "I only want to know." He recounted to her every detail, including the Valenti girl who was wandering in the stable.

"I see. Then it was an accident. We cannot assign blame in such cases as these," said Mary, trying to help him to feel better. "I planned to go to the Valentis' to deliver a housewarming basket. I will go today to assure them that we do not fault them for the fire."

"But, I really ought to pay for the damages," said John Smith with sad eyes. "I would not feel right otherwise."

"I will not hear any more about it. The old stable was rather outdated anyway and needed to be replaced. Father told me that he planned to build a grander stable with electric lights and plumbing even. Which is what I will do now. You must not concern yourself with the cost coming from your wages."

"Miss Mary—"

Mary interrupted him. "I know what you did for William and the medical clinic in Yorktown. It is no use to insist that you pay for the new stable, for I will never allow it. Because of you, our town will have an accessible doctor which is what it has needed all this while. That puts me and the rest of the town in your debt."

"Thank you," he acquiesced. "If there is anything I may do for you at any time, you need only ask."

"There is one thing you can do, Mr. Smith. Dine with me and the others at mealtime while you are waiting for your new home to be built. It would make me very happy to see you at dinner tonight as the guest of honor."

"As you wish, Miss Mary," he said with a defeated sigh.

When Ethan entered the dining room that night, the girls could hardly take their eyes off of him. He looked dashing in his well-fitted suit and tie as he walked in to find a seat.

"Why Ethan, you are a gentleman!" Mary exclaimed. Ethan turned red and sat down quietly. He felt awkward in these fancy clothes, and even more awkward with the extra attention from the girls.

Abigail was still too embarrassed to look him in the eye, but she managed to steal a few glances at Ethan when he was not looking. She reasoned that it was important for her to look to verify that the suit was altered to fit him properly. It fit very nicely indeed. John Smith then entered the dining room, also wearing a suit. He sat across from Abigail. "Thank you for the clothes, young lady," he said quietly to her while the others were chatting. Abigail nodded and smiled.

Ethan got right to the point. "I think we can keep the carriage horses at the Valentis' barn for now, but we will need to board the other three. There is not enough room for all five."

"Mary wrote to the breeder in Yorktown just this morning to inquire," Clara told him with a smile. While Ethan wore a suit and dined at the table with them, he suddenly seemed more eligible in Clara's eyes than ever before.

John Smith sighed heavily. "I have not had food this good in all my life. I am afraid I have finished already and the rest of you have only just started."

The girls giggled. "Mary told us that you are the guest of honor tonight," said Abigail. "I can ask Catherine for another plate for you, Mr. Smith." With the way that everyone dined and laughed that night, one would hardly know that it was all due to a stable fire.

Just before everyone retired to bed, Mary approached Ethan in the Hall near the bottom of the grand staircase. "Ethan, come with me," she said smiling. "There is something I have wanted to show you for a long time." She took his hand and led him to the closed double doors at the end of the Hall. "Do you remember all those times you would ask me what kind of books my father's library had? Come and see." Mary opened the doors to the massive library and Ethan followed her inside.

"Miss Mary!" he exclaimed. "I cannot believe it. This room is a mansion in itself!" The three crystal chandeliers hanging from the ceiling illuminated the rows upon rows of books before him.

"Did you think that we had quite so many books?" she asked smiling.

Ethan laughed. "I did not know there were so many books in the whole world." He put his hands in his pockets and browsed the bookshelves, trying to read all of the titles at once.

"Father was an avid collector. If the book is in print, chances are it is right here in our library," said Mary proudly.

"Would it be alright if I chose one to read?" asked Ethan hopefully.

"It is what I brought you here to tell you. You may choose any book to read and you may explore this room as often as you wish. I know that Father would be pleased to know that his books were being read by you rather than sitting on the shelf," Mary told him.

"Thank you, Miss Mary. I do not know if I could ever read them all, but I will sure try."

CHAPTER 6

"Mr. Tyler is here to see you, Miss Mary," announced Mrs. Price.

"Very good, please bring him in," replied Mary from the desk in the library. Mr. Tyler was the contractor who arrived that day with plans for the new stable. Mary had been busy with the design and planning the past several days.

"If this revised plan is agreeable to you Miss Davenport, we will begin building right away," said Mr. Tyler.

"That is just what I hoped for. And how long until we can expect it to be finished?"

"With enough laborers, we can have your stable up and running in about thirty days."

"Marvelous. Please begin immediately," Mary ordered. After Mr. Tyler left the house, Mary asked Mrs. Price to send Abigail into the library.

"Good afternoon, Mary," greeted Abigail as she walked in. "How was the meeting with Mr. Tyler?"

"It went perfectly. We should have the new stable ready in thirty days. Oh, I miss my Dolly so much! I cannot wait for this to be done so that we can move on and I can go back to riding every day. I will go with Ethan into Yorktown later today to check on the horses at the ranch," Mary said distractedly while looking through the papers on the desk.

"Do you plan to see William while you are in town?" asked Abigail.

Mary stopped what she was doing and stared at the desk blankly. "William," she whispered. "I have not seen him in ages. I hope he has not forgotten about me."

"I am certain that he has not," smiled Abigail.

"I worry that I might only be bothering him if I do visit. I have been so busy with the estate and plans for the new stable, and I know he is busy as well. Ah yes, that is why I asked Mrs. Price to bring you here. I am afraid that I have neglected our new neighbors, the Valentis. I meant to bring this basket to them days ago and I have forgotten. Would you please see to it that they get the basket today? Also, please convey to them that I do not blame them whatsoever for the stable fire."

"It would be my pleasure, Mary. I have been curious about our new neighbors. I will go ask Clara to meet them with me," replied Abigail.

"Oh, that is a splendid idea. It is fitting that the Valentis should meet at least one of the Davenport sisters. I am glad that you thought of it," said Mary. Abigail could see how busy Mary was, so she took the basket to the entry table in the Hall, then went upstairs to Clara's room.

"Good afternoon, Abigail," Clara greeted her at the door, but she seemed flustered.

"I am going to call on the Valentis now with the welcome basket from Mary. Would you like to meet them with me?"

"Any other time I might, but not now. Nellie is coming over in two days to discuss the voyage and I must be preparing. I cannot believe that we are leaving in four days! Which reminds me, I do need the hem of one of my new dresses taken out. If it wouldn't be too much trouble, can you manage it?"

Abigail smiled. "Of course I will. I am happy for you. You must be very excited about seeing New York and London. I have never been outside of Pennsylvania. I do hope you have a splendid time meeting new friends."

"Yes, I am sure it will be marvelous," said Clara as she searched through her wardrobe.

"Just leave your dress on my bed and I will have it back to you by tomorrow," Abigail said as she left the room.

Ethan was at the Valentis' barn conversing with Phillip. "How are you adjusting to country life?" asked Ethan while retrieving the carriage horses.

"It is different from what I expected. I have a lot to learn. I am not used to being so isolated, that is for certain."

"You must have met the Davenport ladies by now," said Ethan.

"I have only met the one—Miss Abigail."

"You have met Abigail?" asked Ethan in surprise. "She is a companion to Miss Mary Davenport. There is also a Miss Clara Davenport in the house."

"Ah, I see. If they are every bit as kind as Miss Abigail, then I must have the most amiable neighbors of anyone."

"Miss Abigail! Miss Abigail!" cried Gabriella as Abigail approached the house. Gabriella had to pick up and hold the skirt of the dress she wore so she could run to her.

"Good afternoon," Abigail greeted with a smile. "How are you today?"

"I am well. Your dress is so pretty. You have the most beautiful things," said Gabriella.

"Thank you, and you have a lovely dress as well. It looks a bit long for you though. Do you have trouble walking while you wear it?"

"I must pick it off the floor so I do not trip. It is my only dress," Gabriella sighed as she ran her hand down the soft skirt of Abigail's dress.

"I understand what it is like to have only one dress, and it is no fun when it comes time for laundry," Abigail said as Gabriella took her hand. "Are your parents in the house?"

"Mama is not, for she is in Heaven. Papa is at the barn with the horse man," answered Gabriella.

"Oh, I see. Perhaps our mothers are acquainted with each other, because mine is also in Heaven. Will you show me to your papa? I have brought this lovely basket for your family."

"That pretty basket is for us? Hooray!" shouted Gabriella as she led Abigail by the hand to the barn.

Ethan noticed Abigail and Gabriella approaching. "Good afternoon," Ethan said as he smiled at her.

"Oh, good afternoon, Ethan. You must be the horse man that Gabriella has told me about," she said playfully. "Good afternoon, Mr. Valenti. I have brought this basket for you on behalf of the family at Davenport House."

"How kind of you. I see there are candies in the basket," remarked Phillip Valenti.

Gabriella perked up. "Candy?"

"Yes," said her father. "Why don't you take this

basket into our kitchen and you and Donnie may have the candies."

"Hooray!" shouted Gabriella as she ran away with the basket in one hand while carrying her dress in the other.

Abigail smiled as she ran away. "She is a dear girl. Um, Mr. Valenti…"

"Please, call me Phillip," he interrupted with a smile.

"Very well, Phillip. I have noticed that Gabriella's dress is a bit large for her."

Phillip nodded. "I found it at a secondhand store, but they did not have any that fit better."

"I understand. I wonder if you might permit me to change the dress so that it fits her properly. You see, I used to be a seamstress and I have the supplies back at the house."

"What a generous offer. I am afraid I have nothing to give you in return…" Phillip said hesitantly.

"It would be my pleasure. I can bring my sewing kit here and have the dress done by the end of the day, so that Gabriella will not have to go so long without it."

Ethan stood there silently, watching the way Phillip looked at Abigail while they talked. Phillip seemed happy to see her and smiled throughout the conversation. Ethan nearly forgot that he was supposed to be bringing the carriage horses back to the house so that he and Mary could go to town. "I must go," he said suddenly. "Goodbye Abigail, Phillip." Ethan rode away on one horse while holding the reigns of the other alongside him.

Clara found the dress that she wished for Abigail to fix for her. She went into Abigail's bedroom to lay the dress on the bed. Clara had been in that room thousands of times before when it belonged to Mary. It was strange that it should belong to Abigail now and felt so different. Clara noticed a small object displayed on the chest of drawers near the bed. It was a wooden carving of a horse. Clara felt her heart sink as she picked up the carving and turned it over to look at all the sides. She instantly knew who it was from. Clara put the wooden horse back on the chest and left the room, still carrying the dress that she had intended to leave for Abigail.

Mary and Ethan were on their way back from the Yorktown ranch where the horses Dolly, Silver and Amethyst were boarding. Mary told Ethan that she would first look into a shop and afterward visit William at the clinic. Ethan secured the carriage horses, then went in to see William himself.

William smiled when he saw him. "Ethan! What a surprise. How good it is to see a familiar face. How is Mary—and the others?" he stammered. He was embarrassed that he could not remember their names just then.

"Everyone is well. I have arrived with Miss Mary just now. She will be in to see you in a few moments," Ethan told him.

"Mary is coming here? Oh, I see," William said nervously as he straightened his shirt and ran his hand through his hair. "So what is the news of Davenport House? I feel so out of touch now."

"The biggest news is that the stable caught fire and burnt to the ground. No one was hurt and all the horses were out, so I suppose that is the good news."

"But where are you and your father living now?" William asked in concern. Now he felt even worse for taking John's money for the clinic.

Ethan sighed heavily. "We are staying in the grand house with the girls."

William chuckled and decided that he did not feel so bad after all. "Mary is generous, of course. At least everyone is alright."

"We also have new neighbors living in the farmhouse where you and Pa used to live," Ethan said quietly.

"How do you like them?"

"Alright, I suppose," muttered Ethan, looking at the floor.

"That bad, eh?"

"No, it is just that I think the man may have set his sights on…one of the girls in the house," Ethan answered. "He is a widower."

"Is he a good man?"

Ethan shrugged.

"Would you think he was a good man if he did not set his sights on this particular girl?" William asked.

Ethan nodded.

William laughed. "Not Mary, I hope. If it was her, I would close up the clinic this instant and—" He was interrupted by Mary knocking at the door. William cringed. "Don't tell her I said that," he whispered as he went to answer the door.

"Good evening," Mary said, smiling brightly when she saw William's face.

"I will be waiting in the carriage, Miss Mary," said Ethan, and he went out the door.

"William, it looks wonderful in here. I see that the new beds are set up now. How have you been?" asked Mary.

"Busy," laughed William. "I hear you have been busy as

well after the stable fire. I am sorry, Mary. You must miss your riding very much."

"I do. I have just been to see Dolly. Mr. Shelton is taking fine care of her and the others at the ranch. When will you buy your motor car?"

"I plan to go to Philadelphia on Friday. I am a little stumped as to how I will manage to return my horse to Yorktown while I am driving the car back," he answered. "I will still need my horse for the more remote house calls here."

"Our driver can take you to Philadelphia in the carriage," Mary offered.

William looked pleasantly surprised. "Well, that would be a perfect solution! If you are certain that you can spare the carriage for the day?"

"I will instruct our driver to come to you on Friday morning and the carriage will be yours for the day. Clara will also be leaving that day—"

Mary was interrupted by a knock at the door of the clinic. William smiled. "I really do need to put an 'OPEN' sign in the window so that folks know they may just walk in." When he opened the door, a woman dressed in poorly patched clothing stood there holding a little boy.

"You the new doctor? Can you help him?" the woman asked William anxiously.

"Yes Ma'am, I am Dr. Hamilton. Bring him inside and I will see how I can help."

Mary smiled at William and left the clinic quietly while he attended to the patient.

Abigail returned to the Valentis' house with her sewing kit, along with her own hairbrush, and the ribbons that her birthday gifts had been wrapped in. Gabriella sat bundled up in a quilt on the children's bed while Abigail worked on the dress. Gabriella and Donnie were fascinated by her sewing and would stand so close to watch that Abigail had to gently remind them to step back more than once. Abigail discovered that there was so much material in the over-sized dress that she would be able to make two dresses from it with more to spare. She skillfully set about making a plain dress for Gabriella, then used the extra material to create ruffles on the sleeves and skirt of the second dress.

Gabriella beamed when she wore her new party dress. She ran to show her father who was in the kitchen, then came back to Abigail in the bedroom. "I don't need to carry this dress when I walk. Thank you, Miss Abigail," Gabriella said, smiling as she twirled around and watched the ruffles flutter.

"It is almost my dinner time, so I must be leaving soon," Abigail told her. "But first I will put this pretty ribbon in your hair."

"Will my hair be in braids?" Gabriella asked excitedly while climbing into Abigail's lap.

"Why, yes. All of the little girls where I grew up wore braids in their hair," Abigail said as she brushed Gabriella's hair and braided it down each side.

"Braid my hair too, Miss Abigail?" asked Donnie.

"Your hair is a little short to braid, but I will brush your hair with this soft hairbrush just the same."

Donnie smiled and waited his turn patiently. When Gabriella's hair was finished, she ran her fingers down the braids over and over to feel the smooth pattern. Donnie closed his eyes and smiled while he sat in Abigail's lap and had his hair brushed. Abigail could hear the sound of clanging dishes and Phillip muttering from the kitchen. She gathered her things and said goodbye to the children.

"Are you alright, Phillip?" she asked him. The smoke filling the room from the oven already answered her question.

Phillip tried to smile. "Just making supper," he said casually as he scrambled to retrieve the food before it burnt even more. Abigail opened a window to let in fresh air. Gabriella and Donnie went into the kitchen.

Gabriella sighed heavily then whispered to Abigail, "Papa always burns our supper."

Abigail smiled. "I should not interrupt your supper. Goodnight, Children. Goodnight, Phillip," she said as she left the house. She could see Ethan walking over to the barn just then with the carriage horses.

"Good evening," she said smiling.

Ethan looked up in surprise. "Abigail—you have been here all this while?"

"I have. I am just leaving for the house now to change for dinner," she replied a little weary.

"I see. I will be just a moment returning the horses, then I can walk to the house with you."

Abigail nodded and offered to help. They secured the horses in the barn, then walked back to Davenport House together. At the dinner table that night, Mary seemed to be quiet and thoughtful. She was secretly disappointed that she could not have visited with William for longer at the clinic. Their friendship started out so strong in the beginning, yet now it almost felt as if they were strangers.

CHAPTER 7

Mr. Tyler arrived at Davenport House the next day with laborers and building materials. They began to work on the new stable right away. Mary met with Mr. Tyler and they conversed for most of the afternoon. Clara had bought many new dresses and accessories and was sorting through them for her upcoming voyage. Ethan and John Smith worked on the estate grounds together. Abigail spent another day at the Valentis' house with the children, since Mary was occupied with the new stable construction. Everyone arrived at dinner that night weary from the day's events and they retired to their beds soon after.

Ethan decided that the bed in the room was too soft for him. He was deep in thought and getting ready to sleep on the floor when he heard a knock at his door. He got dressed quickly and went to answer it.

"Clara," he whispered. "I was not expecting you."

"Well, who were you expecting?" she asked wryly.

"I was not expecting anyone really. What is it?"

"I thought I could come in and talk to you for a while. Like old times," she answered

"It is late. What if one of the servants sees you coming into my room at night?"

Clara shrugged. "Does it matter? I am leaving in three days anyway."

"It matters to me. Go back to bed and we can talk in the morning."

Clara could feel tears welling in her eyes. "I know that I told Nellie I would go with her to London, but all along I have been hoping that you would try to stop me. Why haven't you?"

"I am not going to stop you from going, Clara. You must do with your life as you see fit now."

"But I want you," Clara said as she looked into his eyes. "Say the word and I will stay here, with you."

Abigail was in her bedroom thinking that she would like a walk in the cool night air before she retired to bed. She put on her sweater and opened the door to leave her room, but she could see Clara further down the hallway, whispering with Ethan at his bedroom door. Abigail did not step out into the hallway but instead closed her door and stayed in her room. She could hear her heart pounding in her ears while she tried not to think the worst about what she saw. Then she heard Ethan's bedroom door close. Abigail took a deep breath and opened her door again to look into the hallway. There was no one in sight. Abigail quickly walked out to the grand staircase. Now she wanted to leave for the fresh air even more than before.

Ethan was lying on his bedroom floor when he heard soft footsteps in the hallway. He hoped that Clara had not come back. When it was quiet afterward, Ethan opened his door just in time to see Abigail walking down the staircase to the Hall. He heard the front door open and close and decided that he would also go out. When he first stepped outside, he could see the silhouette of Abigail pacing back and forth not far from the house. Then a figure of a man approached her from the distance. Ethan watched as the man went to speak with Abigail, then the two of them hurried away from the house in the direction of the Valentis' land. Ethan wished that he could go for a ride through the fields right now to think. The new stable could not be completed soon enough.

As soon as Abigail entered the Valentis' house with Phillip, she could hear the children whimpering from the bedroom. "I am sorry to take you away from the house. I did not know what to do. They would not stop crying and said they must see Miss Abigail," explained Phillip.

"It is alright. I am afraid that the children and I have become attached these past days. The poor dears. I will go to calm them just this once, but I must explain that I cannot come every time," Abigail said quietly as she went to the children's bedroom.

"Gabriella, Donnie, whatever is the matter?" she asked gently when she saw them.

"Bad dreams," cried Donnie from the bed. Gabriella nodded in agreement.

"Oh, I am sorry you have had bad dreams. Your papa is here, and he is big and strong and will protect you tonight."

"But we want you, Miss Abigail. Please don't go. We will have more bad dreams if you do," Gabriella begged.

"I have just come to see that you are alright, but I

cannot stay. I must return to my own house, and you must sleep in your own bed." The children continued to whimper. Abigail sighed. "Alright, just this once I will stay until you fall asleep. But you must realize that I cannot come back to do this again and you must learn to sleep on your own."

"Yes, Miss Abigail," they said sleepily as they laid back down. Abigail sat on their bed next to them, watching the children close their eyes, and feeling her own eyelids growing very heavy.

Abigail sat up suddenly in the children's bed. She could see rays of light from the rising sun piercing through the window. She gasped as she realized that she had fallen asleep next to the children all night. She quietly slipped out of the room and ran back to Davenport House. She did not want to face Mrs. Price at the front door, so she opted for the servants' entrance, thinking that she had only minutes before the servants would awake and begin their day. Abigail quietly went up the servants' stairs then hurried down the hallway to her bedroom. She changed into her nightclothes and lay upon her bed, hoping that she could sleep a little longer before having to start the day. She would need to join the girls that afternoon to meet with Nellie Whitmore, who was coming to discuss the voyage with Clara.

"I wonder why Abigail has not come down to breakfast," Mary thought aloud at the dining table. "I hope she is not feeling ill."

Ethan began to worry and looked down at his plate. He had paced outside the house for hours the night before, waiting for Abigail to return. He never saw her come back.

"I am almost feeling ill myself," said Clara, looking down at her breakfast that had not been touched.

"It is likely only butterflies that you have. I always get them just before leaving for an exciting destination. I have not been to New York in ages. Perhaps when I purchase an automobile for the house, we may go every month if we wish. Did you know that William is going to Philadelphia on Friday to buy one for himself? The same day you are leaving for New York, Clara."

Ethan looked up suddenly. "How will he get his horse back to Yorktown?" he asked.

"I have offered William our driver and carriage for the whole day so that his horse may stay in Yorktown while he is away," explained Mary.

"I can take William to Philadelphia," Ethan offered quickly. "I can ensure the carriage horses do well on the journey. I have not had much to do here since we boarded the horses at the ranch, and I am anxious to feel useful again."

"Oh! If you want to, Ethan, of course you should. William will likely enjoy your company more than that of our driver anyway. And our driver will be glad to have the day off. Oh my, it will feel strange being stranded here without a single horse all day," Mary said. "I cannot wait for the stable to be finished."

After breakfast, Ethan thought about knocking on Abigail's door to make sure that she made it back to the house alright. He first stopped at the open door of his room to go inside, but the housemaids were in there making up his bed. He could hear loud giggling and conversation from where he stood just outside the doorway.

"And then she sneaked up the servants' stairs to go back to her bedroom…wearing the *same clothes* she wore last night!" Cecelia said gleefully. "Oh my, was her hair a mess! Not very fitting for a lady's companion. She thought that no one saw her, but I did. Then again, she *did* work at a hotel before, where handsome gentlemen must have rented rooms all the time…"

Ethan's heart was racing. He knew that he must speak to Abigail as soon as possible. He waited for the maids to leave the upstairs, then he went to knock on Abigail's door.

"Good morning, Ethan," she answered cheerfully.

"Good morning," he replied. "The girls were worried when you did not come down for breakfast."

"Oh, I am afraid that I overslept. I was just about to go down to the kitchen to see if there is any breakfast left over."

Ethan looked into her eyes and said seriously, "I must speak with you before you do."

"What is it?" she asked worriedly. She hoped that everyone in the house was alright.

"You must not go to the Valentis' house anymore, the way you have been. It is not safe."

"I do not understand. The Valentis are harmless," replied Abigail.

"I am just worried for you. You have only just met Phillip. You cannot stay at his house all night," whispered Ethan.

Abigail held her breath. "Why do you say I was there all night? Did you follow me?"

"I saw you go outside after dinner. I went to talk to you but saw you meet with Phillip there in the dark," Ethan replied.

Abigail tried to keep her composure, even though she was greatly upset by what he implied. "The children have lost their mother, Ethan. Of all people, I would expect *you* to understand," she said firmly.

Ethan was caught off-guard with her comment. "Do you mean to say that you were with the children all night?"

"Of course I was with the children! Why else would I have gone?" she questioned him daringly.

"Oh Abigail, you should have been more careful! Even the servants are talking about it now," Ethan said sorrowfully.

"What do you mean? What has been said?" she asked in a hoarse whisper.

It pained Ethan to repeat the words. "One of the maids said that she saw you secretly take the servants' stairs early this morning...and that you wore the same clothes you wore yesterday."

Abigail gasped. "Oh dear! Does Mary know?" Abigail sat on her bed slowly, despising every word of this conversation.

"I don't think she knows. She has been busy with the estate. You must be mindful of your time with the Valentis from now on. Then perhaps last night will remain nothing more than servants' gossip."

"Will you tell Mary?"

He shook his head. "She will hear nothing from me." Just then, Ethan could hear Nellie Whitmore's arrival being announced at the front door. "I will leave you now. Miss Whitmore is here." He left down the hallway while Abigail remained where she was, staring blankly ahead of her.

Nellie, Mary, Clara, and Abigail seated themselves in the upstairs sitting room. "I have brought some pictures showing the inside of our ship. It is so charming! You must see the grand staircase, Mary," Nellie chatted excitedly while passing the pictures to the girls.

Abigail tried to smile. She noticed that Clara also seemed to be having difficulty socializing, but Abigail could not think why when she had such a grand trip ahead of her. Nellie continued, "Oh, I cannot wait to leave for New York. I even reserved box seats for us at Wallack's Theater on Broadway. We will see a splendid play the night before we leave! Do you know of *A Midsummer Night's Dream*?"

Clara suddenly spoke up. "Nellie, I am terribly sorry, but I am afraid that I will not be able to accompany you after all." The whole room went silent for a moment.

"I do not understand. Has something happened?" asked Nellie in confusion.

"My mother will not allow me to go. She has been sick with worry ever since I mentioned the voyage, and I do not wish for her to be tormented any further," Clara explained.

Nellie looked down in disappointment. "This is dreadful. I have already sent a telegram to Aunt Lucinda about my bringing a companion. I was looking forward to having the company. Oh, I do not want to spend six whole days alone," she pouted.

"I did think of a solution just last night," Clara told her confidently. "Abigail may accompany you in my place. She would make a marvelous companion for you, and she has never been outside of Pennsylvania." Mary and Abigail looked on in disbelief at Clara's suggestion.

"Well, I would be happy to have you, dear Abigail, but only if Mary can spare you," Nellie said kindly.

"I think we must leave the decision to her," Mary said

hesitantly. "I will be quite busy with the estate while the new stable is being constructed. Abigail is free to go with you…if she wishes."

Another awkward silence followed as they all looked at Abigail for her response. "I am honored that you would consider taking me with you, Nellie. I will go, if it is what you and Mary wish."

Shortly before dinner, Ethan walked around the building site of the new stable to see the progress. It was coming together more quickly than he had anticipated and looked as though it would be quite nice when it was finished. He was surprised to see Abigail slowly walking toward the house from the direction of the Valentis' land. When Abigail saw Ethan approaching her, she looked down and continued walking.

"Have you just come from the Valenti house?" Ethan asked gently.

"Please do not scold me. I only went so that I could tell the children goodbye," said Abigail with tears in her eyes.

"I should not have said those things to you. I was worried and I did not handle it as I should have. You do not need to stop seeing the children on account of what I said," Ethan said apologetically.

"It is not because of that. Clara has decided not to take the voyage after all, and I will accompany Nellie in her place."

"What?" whispered Ethan as he stopped walking. "Clara is staying here at the house?"

Abigail nodded. "You must be pleased to hear it."

"I am surprised. She seemed rather set on going. But

Abigail, do you wish to go with Miss Whitmore, or do you think that you have to?"

Abigail tried to be as honest as possible. "I have felt redundant in my position here as Mary's companion. Mary appointed me before she knew that she would have a sister to keep her company. She also has William for a friend now. I cannot tell if she wishes to have me any longer or is only keeping her word to me. She did not argue when Clara suggested that I go to London with Nellie. I do not wish to be in anyone's way here. Perhaps it is better for all of us if I leave Davenport House."

CHAPTER 8

Abigail looked sadly at the closed traveling case on her bed. It held all of her belongings which did not even fill the case halfway. Today was the day that Abigail and Nellie would leave for New York. The Lusitania would begin boarding the following morning. Abigail was certain that she was not fashionable enough for London. She began to wish that she had never agreed to go, but she did not know how to decline when it seemed to be what the others wanted for her.

"Are you ready for me to take your case, Miss Abigail?" asked Fiona from the doorway.

"Yes, thank you, Fiona," she answered. Fiona took the case downstairs, and Abigail sat on the bed clutching her stomach.

"Abigail," Ethan's voice whispered from the doorway. "Are you alright?"

"It is only butterflies I am sure," she answered tearfully.

Ethan entered the room and knelt in front of her to look up into her eyes. "You don't have to do this. You should only go today because it is what you wish to do, not because you think you have to."

"I do have to. I made a promise and I cannot go back on my word," she said.

Ethan sighed. "I had thought the same once about a promise I made. And it was a mistake from the beginning." They could hear Nellie's arrival being announced downstairs.

"I must go now. I wish you the best with everything. Goodbye, Ethan." Abigail went to meet Nellie at the front door. Ethan watched from Abigail's bedroom window as Nellie's motor car drove away from the house with Abigail in the backseat. He suddenly felt ill at the thought that he may never see her again.

"Ethan, what are you doing in here?" asked Mary from the hallway behind him. "William will be expecting you at any moment."

"Oh, I nearly forgot, Miss Mary," said Ethan. "I was watching Miss Whitmore's motor car take Abigail away."

"Abigail has left already?"

Ethan became angry. "Do you mean to tell me that you did not even meet her outside to say goodbye? She thinks that she has to leave because you do not want her anymore, and your not being there to see her off has only confirmed it!"

Mary stood in shock. Ethan had never spoken to her like this before. "I had no idea! Can she truly think that I do not want her?"

"She said she does not feel like she has a place here anymore, now that you have Clara and have been occupied with the estate. She said you did not even object to her leaving for the voyage!"

"Abigail told you these things? I simply did not want to prevent her from what must be the opportunity of a lifetime for a girl like her. That is all. I never dreamed that it might be interpreted this way."

"Well how did you *think* she would interpret it, Mary?" Ethan cried emotionally as he stormed off.

Mary stood in the hallway with her eyes wide and mouth open in disbelief. "What just happened?" she whispered to herself.

Ethan ran all the way to the Valentis' barn to retrieve the carriage horses. He could not wait to get away from the charged atmosphere of Davenport House. There was just something about the house that seemed to affect everyone in it, making it impossible to think clearly or say the right words. Ethan began to wonder if the house was cursed. He was relieved to have an hour to himself during the drive to Yorktown, and felt much better by the time he arrived and saw William. Ethan waved and smiled at him. William was waiting at the entrance of the clinic and smiled in surprise to see Ethan instead of the other driver from the house. "I asked Miss Mary if I could take you to Philadelphia instead. Sorry I am late," Ethan apologized.

"No bother, I have just finished up with a patient a moment ago," William smiled as he climbed into the carriage. "I have been waiting for this day for a long time." He continued to talk cheerfully about the new car he hoped to get and how his practice was going in town. Ethan was grateful for a conversation that could take his mind off of what was happening at the house.

Mary sat solemnly in the dimly lit drawing room, watching the flames flicker in the marble fireplace across from her. It was the first time in a while that she had slowed down enough to have time to think. She thought about how much she missed her father and how horrible this month had been. She wondered if she was only keeping herself busy as a way to cope with her grief. The tears flowed freely as she realized that the grief was still there, only put on hold for moments at a time throughout the day. Mrs. Price entered the room and saw Mary looking sorrowful.

"Is there anything I can do to help you, Miss Mary?" she asked gently as she handed Mary a handkerchief.

Mary sighed as she dried her tears. "I do need help. I did not realize it before now," she said in a low voice. "I have tried to manage the estate alone, and I do not even have the option to ride away my distress as I did before. I now see the the toll it has taken on me and those around me. I no longer know who I am or what I want from life anymore."

"It is normal to feel this way after such a terrible loss, if I may say so, Miss Mary. You have accomplished a great deal these past weeks. I think your father would be proud."

"Thank you for saying so, Mrs. Price. I do not know what I would do without you here," Mary said honestly. "I said to you that we should find a new housekeeper, but it is you who has kept the house together all this while when it had every reason to fall apart."

"It is kind of you to say so," said Mrs. Price smiling. She had never received so great a compliment in her life. "I wonder if I may make a suggestion that would help your situation?"

"Please, tell me anything," answered Mary.

"The new housemaid, Fiona, is a bright girl. She works hard and is more than capable. At first when you gave me the task of finding a new housekeeper, I felt that I could never find a person to meet my own standards. However, Fiona has proved herself beyond my expectations. I believe she could be the one."

"Fiona? She looks very young. How old is she?" asked Mary curiously.

"She is sixteen, Miss Mary. But do not let her age fool you. She is wise beyond her years and the hardest worker I have seen. I believe she will do the job to your satisfaction."

"A high recommendation indeed. But how does this help with my situation?" asked Mary.

"I believe what you need is an overseer for the estate. Someone to act as a land steward, who would manage the accounts and meet with Mr. Tyler about the stable construction. With an overseer in place, you can review the accounts only at your leisure and have time for your friends and your own life. I would like to be considered for this position myself, as I will be managing my daughter's land already. I would still be available to guide Fiona into her new role as housekeeper."

Mary sighed with relief. "An overseer. Why could I not think of it? You have saved me, Mrs. Price. It is a bold move for a woman to take such a position. But if any woman can do it, I am certain it is you. Please, let it be as you say."

Mrs. Price smiled. "Very good, Miss Mary. You may rest tomorrow, and all of next week if that is what you choose. I will see to the finishing of the stable and collecting of the rents." Mary felt as though a weight had lifted off her shoulders.

Nellie and Abigail arrived at The Grand Hotel on Broadway. Abigail was weary from the drive and grateful to check in to a beautiful room to rest. She felt nervous about boarding the ship the next day. She did not know anything about ocean liners, but she could remember that many people had perished aboard a ship called Titanic just three years ago. She shuddered as she thought about how it must have been to freeze in the water while praying for rescue. Abigail was grateful that she at least had pleasant company, and honored that a lady of Nellie's status would want Abigail at all. Perhaps Nellie would take her on as a lady's companion in the future. Everything that Abigail owned was in her travel case, except for the documents and small items that she carried in her purse. She wondered if anyone would notice if she stayed in London and never returned to Davenport House.

Ethan and William arrived in Philadelphia. They found the model of car that William could afford for just under five hundred dollars. Ethan tried not to flinch when he heard the cost. William had told him that five hundred dollars was a modest price for a car, now that these affordable models were being mass produced. "Do you know how to drive this thing?" Ethan asked William.

"I did some driving before I moved to Yorktown. You ready to take it for a spin?" William asked with a grin. Ethan grinned back at him. They drove the car around town for a good while.

William was pleased with his purchase, and Ethan seemed happy simply to have accompanied him to Philadelphia. Before Ethan returned to the carriage, he asked William if they could drive the new car for a little while longer. William obliged and they soon found a scenic road for the drive.

"What is it like living in the grand house with all the girls now?" asked William with a smile.

Ethan buried his face in his hands and shook his head. "Why do you suppose I insisted on coming with you today?"

William threw back his head and laughed. "It cannot be so bad, surrounded by beautiful ladies."

"Well…the food in the dining room is good," Ethan said wryly as he uncovered his face. "I won't be staying for much longer. The new stable will be finished soon."

"I see. And how are things with your…special lady?" William asked carefully.

"I will not see her for a long while," he answered, suddenly appearing downcast. "She was invited on a voyage with Miss Nellie Whitmore."

"A voyage? Where is this supposed to happen?" questioned William.

"Miss Whitmore said they will cross the ocean on a ship called Lusitania, then stay at her aunt's house in London. I suppose Miss Whitmore plans to introduce her into society and the finer things there," Ethan explained sadly.

William felt his heart sinking into his stomach. "Please tell me that they have not already left the house for this voyage," he said with concern in his voice.

"They left for New York just this morning," Ethan replied. William abruptly stopped the car, turned it around, and sped up the road. "What is it? Where are we going?" Ethan asked, startled by the sudden change in course.

"New York," replied William seriously. "We need to stop the girls before they get on that ship."

Mary and Clara dined alone that night. "It is not the same without Abigail," said Mary sadly.

"She will have the time of her life, though. I wish it

could have been me. If only my mother would have let me," said Clara.

"It feels strange to be stranded here without Ethan or any of the horses. We could not go anywhere tonight if we wanted to," remarked Mary.

"Where would you go, if you could?"

"I would see William, of course. I hoped that he might have returned with his automobile and paid us a visit today. I will go to see him tomorrow at the clinic when Ethan returns with our carriage. I should also call on the Valentis tomorrow. What did you think of them?"

"I have not seen them yet," answered Clara.

"Oh dear, I *have* been disconnected. I thought that you went with Abigail already. We should both call on them tomorrow and introduce ourselves properly."

Fiona sat in Mrs. Price's office in disbelief. "You wish—me—to be housekeeper of Davenport House?"

"I believe you will do splendidly. Your wages will double as will your workload. We will take you into Yorktown tomorrow for a suitable dress uniform."

Fiona's eyes grew wide. "Mother will be so pleased. May we please see her while we are in Yorktown? It will mean the world to my family." Fiona could hardly contain her excitement, and could not entirely believe that what Mrs. Price told her could be real. Fiona went back to her room in the servants' quarters that she shared with her sister.

"Bridget! I have the most wonderful news. I am to be the new housekeeper of Davenport House!" she exclaimed to her sister.

"It cannot be! What is to happen with Mrs. Price?" asked Bridget.

"I could not believe it either, but Mrs. Price has just told me that she is to be the new overseer and will transfer her position as housekeeper to me! We must be extra vigilant to do well so we do not let her down. Oh, I cannot wait to tell Mother!"

"I am afraid that Cecelia will not take this news well. She has been here for years and will not like being looked over for a promotion," Bridget reasoned.

"You may be right. I will manage the transition as best I can without upsetting her."

The doorman held the door for Nellie and Abigail as they exited The Grand Hotel. Wallack's Theater was directly next to the hotel, so the girls walked right up to the crowded entrance, then up the stairs to their reserved box seat. Abigail was beginning to feel exhilarated from the experience. She felt her heart beating faster in anticipation as the lights dimmed and the opening act began, bringing a hush over the excited audience. Abigail could not see the stage very well, but she already knew that the music and colors were spectacular. "Abigail dear," Nellie said softly while nudging her. "Use your opera glasses." Abigail was glad that she could not be seen blushing under the dim theater lights. She held the opera glasses in front of her eyes as she observed Nellie doing in the seat next to her. The stage suddenly came to life with flowing costumes and enchanted scenery. Abigail remembered Mrs. Stein, the woman who used to employ her as a seamstress. Mrs. Stein would often rave about the Broadway plays she had seen, but until this moment, Abigail could not quite envision what her employer spoke of. Abigail thought that the fairy costumes on stage were nothing short of divine. She continued to feel her senses gratified for the duration of the play.

As the themes of love, jealousy, and elopement played out in front of her eyes, Abigail could not help but think about Ethan and Clara back at Davenport House. If they were truly engaged, why had they not announced it? Clara could do as she pleased now that she was a Davenport. And why did it feel as though Ethan had affections for Abigail? She could feel her own heart melt and knees go weak every time he smiled at her. If she did not know any better, she would think that Ethan was in love with her instead of with Clara.

Abigail became mesmerized with the play during the final acts when it was announced that the whole of the pleasurable evening may have only been a dream. Abigail tried to put thoughts of Clara and Ethan out of her mind. She realized her life may now be headed for a different future than she had thought only days ago. The audience stood up and clapped with fervor as the actors bowed on the stage, signaling the end of *A Midsummer Night's Dream*. Abigail wondered if this new life with Nellie may not be so bad after all.

CHAPTER 9

I t was Saturday, the first of May, the day that Nellie and Abigail would begin their voyage across the ocean. Abigail wore her pink dress with pink hat, along with her only jacket. Nellie wore a dark skirt and jacket with a costly fur stole draped around her shoulders and a matching muff for her hands. Abigail could hardly believe her eyes when she saw the enormous ship that would be their hotel for the next week. Nellie had told her that it was the largest passenger ship in the world, but Abigail did not realize just how large until it loomed high before them, even from a distance. They arrived at Pier 54 where they were met by porters who took their luggage. All that Abigail had with her now was the purse that she carried, which contained her documents and a little wooden horse.

"This way for the first-class passengers, Abigail," Nellie said as she led her new friend to the correct boarding area. Abigail looked at the many people around her. The men were in their hats and jackets, shaking hands with the other passengers and some speaking to the crew. Many of the women were holding small children and waiting their turn to board. Abigail wondered how such a voyage would be handled by small children, when she felt this afraid to board the imposing ship herself. She had never been on a ship or even seen a pier before. She had only seen the pictures from Nellie, but this was far more grand than she imagined. She took deep breaths, trying to calm down. Some of the passengers appeared just as nervous as Abigail, while others like Nellie looked confident and eager to begin their voyage. Abigail felt like she wanted to run back to the safety of The Grand Hotel, but she knew that now of all times, it was too late to change her mind.

"Fiona is to be housekeeper?" Cecilia cried incredulously. "Why haven't I been asked? I have been here for longer!"

Mrs. Price sighed heavily. "Fiona is to be the housekeeper and I will be overseer to the estate. If you do not like these changes, you are free to take your things and find work elsewhere."

Cecelia continued to scowl as she sat at the table in the servants' quarters. Mrs. Price and Fiona walked away. "I will have a hard time with that one. I can already see it," remarked Fiona to Mrs. Price.

"You must be able to stand up to her and be firm. Do not let her bully you," said Mrs. Price. "The horses have not yet returned, so I am afraid we must postpone the trip to Yorktown for your uniform. A maid uniform will have to do for today."

"And you are certain that Miss Mary is agreeable to my being the new housekeeper?" asked Fiona hesitantly.

"I am certain. I have given her the highest recommendation of you and I know that you will live up to it."

"Of course, Mrs. Price. Thank you."

Pier 54 in New York was teeming with excited travelers. William and Ethan did not know which hotel Nellie and Abigail had gone to, so they rented a room the night before and arrived at the pier in the morning with hopes of finding them. Over a thousand passengers were waiting to board the majestic Lusitania. William and Ethan looked urgently through the crowd for the girls. Then they found the first-class boarding line. Ethan felt like his heart stopped when he saw a beautiful young woman in a pink hat and dress. "I see them!" he exclaimed to William just before he ran through the crowd shouting. "Abigail!"

Abigail was with Nellie, waiting to show their documents to the attendant at the front of the line. They were nearly to the stairs that would lead to the ship and she could feel her stomach twisting into knots. She thought that she heard a voice calling her name, but so much noise came from the crowd that Abigail thought it must be her imagination, or someone calling another girl with the same name. Just before reaching the attendant who would take their documents, Abigail was certain that she heard someone calling her name again. She turned around and looked into the crowd. The guards on the pier were stopping a man from reaching the first-class passenger line.

"Land sake's!" she gasped. "Nellie! Ethan is here!" She pointed him out to Nellie.

"What on earth is Ethan doing here?" Nellie asked as she let the passengers behind them board the ship. "I will hold our place here. Go see what he wants, quickly."

Abigail ran to Ethan where the guards were warning him to not bother the first-class ladies. "Please, I know this man, let me speak with him," she said gently to the guards. The guards walked away and Ethan and Abigail were left to talk.

"This ship is not safe, Abigail. William said it is a target for the War and we came here to stop you and Miss Whitmore from getting on," he urged with wide eyes.

Abigail held her hand over her stomach when Ethan said the words. She had heard some other passengers murmuring about the War, and she felt ill every time it was mentioned. "But they have already taken our cases. We cannot get them back now," Abigail said worriedly.

William joined them from the crowd just then. "Leave the cases," he urged. "Your lives are more important. You must persuade Nellie to leave the pier immediately and come back with us." Abigail nodded and returned to Nellie who waited in bewilderment near the stairs to the ship.

"Is that Mary's Dr. Hamilton?" asked Nellie in surprise. "I cannot imagine what he can be doing here just now."

Abigail tried to speak with Nellie discreetly. "They have come to stop us. Dr. Hamilton said that our ship is a target for the War and we are putting our lives at risk by boarding it today."

"Oh, all of the rumors," Nellie said casually. "Dear Abigail, they would not continue with this voyage if it was unsafe. Look at all of these people. Do you think that they would board the ship if they believed those rumors? We needn't worry. The crew know what they are doing."

"I really think we should listen to them," said Abigail in concern.

"Oh, I will go to talk to Dr. Hamilton myself. Hold our place in line so that we may board in a moment." Nellie went over to William and Ethan who stood a distance away to wait for them. "You two are scaring poor Abigail," she scolded. "Why have you come all this way today when you never objected before?"

William looked her in the face solemnly. "The German Embassy has warned Americans not to sail on this ship. Some suspect that there are weapons aboard being transported to Great Britain, which makes your ship a target. I beg of you not to go. Postpone your journey for another time when it is safe."

"I cannot postpone. It has all been arranged. I am afraid you have wasted your trip here. We will not be in London very long," she assured him with a smile. "You will see us again in no time."

"Miss Whitmore," said Ethan anxiously. "Abigail will do whatever you say, even if it means putting her life at risk. If you will not listen to us, you must make it clear that it is *her* choice whether to go with you."

Nellie was touched by their concern, but she reasoned that the ship would not have boarded the passengers if what William and Ethan said was true. She went back to Abigail who stood waiting for her anxiously. "I am going to board now, Abigail. You must decide whether to go with me or go back to Davenport House with the men. I know that the doctor is worried for us, but I think he is overly cautious. Still, you must do what your heart tells you and not worry whose feelings you may hurt," Nellie spoke compassionately. Abigail nodded. The girls got back in line and showed their documents to the crew. Ethan and William looked on in sorrow.

Abigail took the first step onto the stairs. "Wait!" she cried. "Nellie, I can't. I am sorry!"

"Do what you must, Dear. Do not worry about me," said Nellie kindly as she kissed Abigail on the cheek. Abigail left the boarding area and went back to William and Ethan.

"Please take me home. I am afraid that I am ill," she said to them tearfully as she felt her knees give out from under her.

Cecelia pouted as Fiona gave orders to the household staff that day. "Cecelia, are you listening?" Fiona asked suddenly, interrupting the girl's daydreaming.

"I am sorry, *Miss Fiona*. I suppose I am just not used to taking orders from housemaids," Cecelia answered daringly, looking Fiona up and down.

Fiona appeared unaffected. "If you were listening, you would have heard that you are now attending to Miss Mary and Miss Clara in their rooms while Bridget will take on the bulk of the cleaning work."

Cecelia perked up at this news. It was not a promotion as grand as housekeeper, but to be so close to the Davenport sisters was a position to be envied. "Gladly, *Miss Fiona*," she answered.

Mary and Clara were about to go into the dining room for lunch. Mrs. Price was taking Fiona through the house explaining various duties while Fiona nodded willingly. "Mrs. Price?" asked Mary. "Has Ethan not returned with the carriage?"

"He has not, Miss Mary," answered Mrs. Price.

Mary looked disappointed. "I wonder what can be taking him so long. I do hope the horses have done well on the journey."

"Are we still going to see the Valentis today?" asked Clara.

"Yes, I believe we must. We have neglected them for too long. I have asked Catherine to make up some sweets and cakes for us to bring. At least the children are certain to like us," Mary said with a giggle. "But I am afraid that I have neglected William as well. I would go to see him and his new automobile today if only the carriage was here. I hope he knows I have not forgotten him."

Ethan carried Abigail in his arms to a place away from the crowd. William went to find something for her to eat and drink. "I am sorry, I do not know why I could not walk any longer," Abigail apologized to Ethan.

Ethan smiled at her and kissed her forehead. "I was relieved enough to see you returning to us that I would have carried you all the way back to Davenport House. I thought I might die when I saw you boarding that ship," he whispered.

"I had the most dreadful feeling all of a sudden when my foot touched the first step. It was the same feeling I had the day when I learned my mother had influenza. I could not take another step. I was grateful that you and William were there waiting for me. I do not know what I would have done otherwise."

William returned with food and drink for Abigail. He looked very serious as he watched the travelers still at the pier waiting to board. "All of those people," he said under his breath. "I hope to God that I am wrong." He watched Abigail carefully as she ate and drank, and the color gradually returned to her face. They could hear shouts of "bon voyage" as the Lusitania raised her flag and slowly pulled away from the pier. William had hoped all this while that he might see Nellie and other passengers turn back from the boarding line at the last minute. He had tears in his eyes as he watched the ship sail. He then turned to Abigail and said in a low voice, "We must get you home so that you may rest in bed. You are understandably shaken from the day's events." They climbed into William's new car and drove away from New York. Ethan sat with Abigail in the backseat, holding her hand all the way to Philadelphia.

Mary and Clara walked to the Valentis' house with their offering of sweets and cakes. Gabriella answered the door of the farmhouse in her new ruffled dress. "Papa, there are ladies at the door!" she yelled through the house. Mary and Clara giggled. A man dressed in work clothes came to the door.

"Good afternoon," he greeted them.

"Good afternoon," Mary replied. "You must be Mr. Valenti. We are your neighbors. I am Mary Davenport and this is my sister, Clara."

"I am pleased to meet your acquaintance. I am Phillip Valenti. My girl who answered the door is Gabriella, and I have another little one in the house called Donnie."

"We are pleased to make your acquaintance as well," replied Mary. "Is Mrs. Valenti home?" Phillip Valenti looked down at the floor and Mary knew at once that she had made a mistake.

"Mrs. Valenti is no longer with us," he said sadly. "It is only me and the children. We have lately moved here from Pittsburgh."

"I see," said Mary. She felt tears stinging her eyes as she thought about her own father who was no longer with her. She tried to keep the subject light. "And how are you enjoying life in the country, Mr. Valenti?"

He chuckled. "It is an adjustment, Miss Davenport," he answered.

"We have brought these sweets for you and the children," offered Clara. "Perhaps you may join us for dinner tonight? We will dine at 7 o'clock."

"How kind of you. We are honored," he smiled. "Will Miss Abigail be at dinner? Or has she left for her voyage?"

"She left only yesterday morning," replied Mary.

"I see," he answered. "Miss Abigail has been a tremendous help to me and the children. I was sorry to see her go."

Mary smiled to remember Abigail's kind nature and suddenly felt sad that she had really gone. "I hope we may all become good friends," she said to Phillip. "We will be glad to see you tonight at dinner."

William, Abigail, and Ethan arrived in Philadelphia where Ethan would retrieve the carriage. Abigail walked with Ethan while William conversed with the automobile dealer. "You will be home long before I am," Ethan said to Abigail. "I hope you may rest when you get there."

"I do not know how I will rest. I am afraid to face Mary again," confessed Abigail.

"I am afraid to face her too, but for different reasons. You must not be afraid, Abigail. Miss Mary loves you a great deal. I believe she will be happy to have you as her companion once more."

"That is not all I am worried about. When I first became Mary's companion, she took me shopping at a department store and bought me many fine dresses and things. But everything I own is now in my traveling case on the Lusitania. I will be down to only one dress again, with nothing to wear to dinner. I will not even have my sewing kit anymore. I am afraid that I do not make a proper lady's companion in any respect."

"I am sorry about your belongings, Abigail. I understand the feeling of losing everything in a single day," said Ethan sadly.

"Of course you do…with the fire. I had forgotten about that for a moment. I will need to save my allowance to be able to buy new dresses…if Mary still wants me. I have sent all of my wages to my family in Johnstown. Oh I wish I was not so nervous about going back," Abigail thought aloud, trying to take deep breaths.

Ethan looked into her eyes. "Miss Mary will be glad to see you return. And I am glad for your return…knowing that you are safe in the house, and not aboard that ship." He looked at her intently like he had more to say.

"Are you ready to return home, Abigail?" asked William, walking toward them.

"I am ready. I will see you later at the house, Ethan. I wish you a safe journey." Abigail and William left in the car and Ethan started his long ride home in the carriage. He thought about what he would say to Mary when he returned.

It was nearly time to change for dinner. Mary was concerned that Ethan had still not returned with the carriage. She went out the front door and watched for awhile, wondering what she could do with no way to get to town. Cecelia went to attend to Clara before dinner.

"Cecelia," Clara smiled when she saw her former workmate enter the bedroom. "I have not seen you in ages. How do you like my new room?"

"It is beautiful, Miss Clara. You fit in quite well. Why, it was only weeks ago that we were cleaning the house together, and now you are one of the family!" Cecelia squealed. "You have finally received the life that you deserved all this while. Now, I will be attending you, since Fiona is the new housekeeper." Cecelia paused for a moment, then said carefully, "Isn't it a funny thing that Fiona should be promoted so soon after starting here? And at such a young age."

"I suppose it does seem hasty. After all, you have worked here for longer. I wonder if Mary is aware. I will speak to her about it, if you wish," Clara offered.

"Oh, that is so very kind of you, Miss Clara. I do not wish to cause trouble," Cecelia said innocently. "Now let us see what we can do with your lovely hair tonight." Cecelia continued to flatter Clara as she dressed her for dinner.

Mary was just about to go back into the house when she heard the sound of a motor car coming up the drive. Her heart began to beat faster. She hoped that William was coming to see her. She smoothed her hair and dress and waited near the driveway to meet him as he drove up.

"William! Abigail?" Mary was surprised and confused when William parked in front of the house. "Has something happened? Abigail, are you too ill to travel? Where is Ethan?"

"Abigail needs to rest tonight, Mary," William started. "Ethan is on his way, but there is more to the story. I will explain everything to you when Abigail gets settled into her room."

"Thank you for everything," Abigail told William as he helped her out of the car. She looked at Mary, then down at the ground. "I am sorry, Mary. I could not go with Nellie. I hope it is alright that I have come back."

Mary walked to Abigail and embraced her. "Davenport House is your home for as long as you wish it to be," Mary told her sincerely. "Let me help you to your bedroom."

William waited for Mary in the Hall. Mary finally came down the stairs and invited William to sit with her in the drawing room. "Abigail is settled in. She seems quite weary from the day," said Mary.

"Yes, she was understandably distressed when we met her at the pier. Ethan and I had to persuade her not to board the ship. Ethan told me of the girls' travel plans when we were in Philadelphia. We went straight to New York to find them and bring them back." William looked down sadly. "Nellie would not return with us."

"But why should they not take the voyage?" Mary asked confused.

"Mary, the world is at war. Germany is at war with Great Britain. Your friends were headed into a war zone. There are also rumors of weapons being aboard the Lusitania. Whether there is truth to these rumors or not, the ship is a target."

Mary's eyes grew wide. "I did not know it was so serious! Oh, poor Nellie. I do hope she arrives in London alright. Now I will be sick with worry until I hear back from her."

"I hope that she will be alright too. I hope that I am wrong in my worries about the ship. I am so sorry, Mary," William said gently. "I tried to stop her but she would not listen."

"I have missed you so much, William," Mary blurted

out. "Please stay and have dinner with us. You have done so much for my friends and for me. I hope you know I have not forgotten you."

"I have missed you too, Mary," he replied in earnest.

Ethan returned that night well after dinner, weary from the day's travels. He put the horses away in the Valentis' barn, then went to the house. He could see Mary standing outside the house speaking with William in the dark. Ethan hung his head when he thought about the apology he owed for how he had spoken to Mary the previous day.

When Mary saw Ethan approaching, she ran to meet him. She threw her arms around his neck and kissed his cheek. "Thank you for going all that way to save my friends," she said to him. "I was so worried about you when you did not return this morning. William has explained everything."

"Is Abigail alright?" asked Ethan.

"She is resting now and had dinner in her room."

Ethan breathed in relief. "Miss Mary, I am sorry for what I said to you. I was never angry with you, only with myself. Please forgive me for speaking to you that way."

"There is nothing to forgive. I was in desperate need of someone in the house being honest with me, and you said exactly what I needed to hear. I have now made some changes that I think will help the house. And I have assured Abigail that this is her home forever if she wishes it."

Ethan could feel tears forming in his eyes. "Thank you, Miss Mary." He went into the house, and William drove back to Yorktown. Nearly everyone in the house was more than ready to retire for the night.

Ethan was beginning to fall asleep on the floor of his

room when a knock at his door startled him awake. He groaned knowing that he would have to get up. He reluctantly pulled his shirt on over his head and stood up to answer the door. "Clara, what are you doing here?"

"I waited all day for you to return. Cecelia just told me that you had already gone to bed, but I had to see you for myself."

"Why, Clara?" Ethan said exasperated. He only wanted to lie down and sleep after the day he had.

"Now we can be together again without any distractions, like before. Abigail is a nice girl, but she cannot make you happy like I can," said Clara quietly. She did not realize that Abigail had returned to the house that very night.

Ethan became upset. "That is why you sent her away, isn't it?"

"I saw the horse carving in her room. You used to give me such gifts all the time. You said that it was because you loved me."

"I was wrong, Clara. I thought what we had was love, but it was only you waiting until something better came along. Whatever it was that we had—it is over. It was over a long time ago. Now please go so I can sleep." Ethan closed the door before she could say anything else. Clara stood in front of the door for a moment while her eyes filled with tears, hoping that he would open the door again. When she could see he was not going to, she hurried away to her room. Cecelia was standing just around the corner. She had heard every word.

CHAPTER 10

Ethan was up at sunrise and went to find his father. John Smith was already in the gardens, working harder than he ever had before. He still felt guilty about the stable fire, and working harder on the estate was the only way he knew how to redeem himself for it.

"Pa, I need to talk to you about something," said Ethan.

"I am glad to see you home safe, Son," replied his father. "What do you need to talk about?" Ethan then explained to him all that had happened in the two days before.

"This is why I needed to talk to you," Ethan continued. "You only need to agree to my idea if you are certain about it yourself. I know it will make all the difference to her, but I would never expect you to say yes if it would be too difficult."

"You are doing the right thing, Son," said his father with tears in his eyes. "You should go to her right away, and know that you have my blessing in what you are about to do."

Fiona and Mrs. Price took the carriage to Yorktown that morning. Fiona found a suitable uniform dress for her position as housekeeper, then went to visit her family to tell them the news of her promotion. Her younger sisters were excited to see her, and her mother was elated when Fiona handed her ten dollars.

"I cannot believe our good fortune," her mother cried with tears of joy. "To think, my own Fiona is housekeeper at Davenport House. Blessed Providence has shown favor on our family! You have made us proud, Daughter!"

Fiona was grateful for her mother's affection, but she was still nervous about going back to the house to deal with Cecelia, who was growing more impertinent with every interaction they had. Fiona hoped that her new uniform dress might help her to look the part and give Cecelia a reason to show respect.

Abigail was feeling much better that morning. She got dressed early and thought about taking a walk outside before breakfast. Just as she was opening her bedroom door to leave, she saw Ethan approaching her, with his arms holding what looked like a large quilt. He seemed nervous when he met her in the doorway.

"Abigail," he said, feeling his heart race in his chest. "I came to give you these." He handed her a bundle wrapped in white linen. Abigail took it to lay on her bed and gasped when she pulled back the linen. Folded neatly inside were five beautiful dresses made with fine material and trimmed in lace.

"Did you buy these in Philadelphia yesterday? They are very beautiful Ethan, but I must pay you back when I have the money," Abigail insisted. She was overwhelmed with emotion and went over to Ethan to hug him.

"You do not need to pay me back," he replied as he hugged her close. "I did not buy them. They were my mother's."

Abigail backed away and looked at Ethan as tears filled her eyes. She did not know what to say, but Ethan knew what she was thinking. "Pa wanted you to have them too. He said that it is alright if you must alter them to fit proper."

Abigail nodded. "I will take very good care of them. Thank you," she said. Ethan smiled at her, then left the doorway before anyone saw him.

Mrs. Price passed Mary on the way to breakfast and smiled at her. "Miss Mary, I have good news. Although the apartment above the stable has yet to be finished, the stalls are complete and the horses may return at any time."

Mary gasped in delight. "This is the most wonderful news of all! I will ride Dolly home today! Ethan and I will go directly after breakfast to buy new saddles and—oh I cannot wait!"

Abigail gazed in delight at her reflection in the full-length mirror. She was wearing one of the dresses that Ethan had given her. It was a dark purple with elegant lace flowing from the elbow length cuff. She did not need to alter the dress at all because it fit perfectly. It was one of the most beautiful dresses she had ever seen. She left her bedroom and observed Clara on the upstairs landing, beginning to walk down the staircase on her way to breakfast.

"Good morning, Clara," Abigail said before Clara noticed that she was behind her. Clara spun around and stared at her. Clara looked as if she had seen a ghost. "What is it? Were you not expecting me?" asked Abigail.

Clara was speechless for a minute, then finally demanded, "How did you get here? Why aren't you with Nellie? I saw you leave in her automobile!"

"William brought me home after persuading me that the ship was unsafe. Nellie did not come back with us though," Abigail said sadly.

"She must have been disappointed that you abandoned her at the last minute," Clara said haughtily. "If I knew that you were going to be so ungrateful for the voyage, I would have gone myself. Who knows if either of us will ever have the chance again." Clara stormed away down the stairs.

Abigail was surprised that Clara spoke to her so rudely. She remembered Clara behaving this way before when she was jealous of Abigail being made a companion to Mary. She did not know that Clara still held such resentment for her, but Abigail guessed that it must have something to do with the attention she was getting from Ethan lately.

She went into breakfast where Mary, Clara, and Ethan were already seated. Ethan could hardly stop looking at Abigail in the new dress. Abigail noticed him looking. Clara noticed it too.

"You look lovely today, Abigail. Are you feeling better?" asked Mary kindly.

"Yes, I do feel much better. Thank you." Abigail sat down and was relieved that Mary ruled the conversation at breakfast. Mary explained the changes to the household staff and plans to bring the horses back today. They would have Ethan, John Smith, and Mary ride the horses home, while the driver returned the carriage to the house. Abigail knew that she wanted to see John Smith before he left, so she finished breakfast early and went into the gardens to look for him.

"Pardon me…Mr. Smith?" she said timidly when she found him kneeling beside the plants in a flower bed. He looked up at her and could not speak. Abigail hoped that she was not upsetting him. "I just wanted to say thank you for your kindness. I thought that you might like to know that I do not have to alter the dresses one bit."

John Smith stood up to face her. He did not say anything, but much to Abigail's surprise, he walked up to her and kissed her on the cheek. Then he went back to the flower bed and kneeled down to tend to the plants. Abigail giggled and returned to the house.

Mary saw the "OPEN" sign on the door of the clinic and walked in. William was wearing a white overcoat and sitting behind a desk. "Mary!" he exclaimed when he saw her. He motioned to the chair in front of him.

"Good afternoon, William. I have just come here with Dolly. We are able to bring the horses to the new stable today," she said beaming.

"I am very happy for you. You look well! Thank you for coming to see me on your way back to the house," he told her.

"I have made some changes to the house. When I tried to do everything by myself, I became overwhelmed and disconnected from the people I loved. Now I have help. Mrs. Price, who used to be the housekeeper, is now overseer of the estate. I have more time to see my friends and I came to invite you to dinner tonight."

"I wish I could, but I have appointments to keep," said William sadly. "It is a doctor's schedule, I'm afraid."

"Of course," said Mary. "Perhaps you could come to dinner tomorrow?"

William shook his head. "I am sorry, Mary."

Mary tried not to panic, but she was worried now

that William might not have cared for her as much as she hoped. She tried one more time. "Why don't I just tell you that you are welcome at the house always, for dinner or just to visit. Perhaps you could come when you have time."

William smiled. "I will do my best. I hope you know that I do want to see you. Only I don't know how to make it happen just now."

Mary smiled too. "I suppose that makes me feel better. At least I don't have to worry that you are avoiding me."

William laughed. "Never. I miss the days of living in the farmhouse and seeing you nearly every day. Please don't give up on me just yet."

Abigail went to the Valentis' house to tell the children that she would not be leaving on a voyage after all. The children were happy to see her, as was their father. She talked to them for a little while before returning to the house. Mary had come home with Dolly not long ago and asked Abigail to accompany her on a ride. Abigail was happy to oblige. She changed her clothes and went out to the stable. Ethan was there getting the new equipment organized.

"We are ready for a ride," Mary said happily as she climbed back onto Dolly.

"Very good, Miss Mary," Ethan answered. Abigail went with him to get the saddle for Amethyst.

"I was able to find your father and thank him this morning," she said quietly.

"Oh yeah? What did he say?"

Abigail giggled. "He did not say anything. He walked up to me and kissed my cheek."

"He did?" Ethan asked incredulous.

Abigail nodded and they both began laughing.

"See how much Amethyst missed you?" Ethan said, smiling as he helped Abigail onto her horse.

Abigail looked at Ethan and smiled back at him. "I missed her too."

Mary and Abigail had an enjoyable ride over the fields. "Mr. Valenti said you have been a big help with the children," Mary remarked.

Abigail blushed. "Those dear children. The little girl had only one dress and it was so big for her that I was able to make two dresses from it. I have been thinking, if you might agree to it, perhaps I may occasionally bring them extra food from our kitchen. I do not think they have much to eat, and Phillip is not much of a cook."

"I am ashamed I did not think of it myself. I will tell Fiona when we return to make sure the Valentis receive from our kitchen. Thank you for saying something. I finally met with the family only yesterday."

"It was good of you to invite them to dine last night. I was sorry to have missed them. Bridget mentioned to me that she took the children to the kitchen to have their dinner there. Fiona must be working out splendidly if she is housekeeper already."

"She does do her job well. The only thing is, I miss her attending to me. Now she has Cecelia attending me, who I do not much care for. I thought to dismiss Cecelia only weeks ago when she assisted Mother in her plot against us. The only reason I kept her on was because we had no other maids."

"Do you need me to help as a maid, Mary?" offered Abigail.

Mary smiled at her. "The best way you can help me is

to stay on as my companion. I love you and trust you. I hope I did not cause you to think that I could do without you when I said you could go with Nellie."

"Thank you for saying so, Mary. I do worry for Nellie. I look forward to hearing that she has arrived safely. The ship is scheduled to arrive in Liverpool in four days. We should not have to wait very long. Either way, I am grateful to your William that he came to rescue us in New York."

Mary smiled shyly. " 'My' William? I wish he was. Sometimes I think he cares for me, but I feel so distant from him now that he is busy with the clinic. I cannot fault him for wanting to help people all day. In fact, I think it only makes me love him more."

Abigail smiled. "You love him, Mary?"

"I do, so much. But I did not mean to say it out loud just then. Please do not tell anyone. It is the first time I have ever felt in love, and I am afraid. He has not expressed that he has any intention toward me. What if he does not feel the same way?"

"I think it is what every person in love is afraid of," said Abigail. Mary smiled and they continued to ride and talk, turning their minds to lighter topics. It was beginning to feel like their friendship was growing stronger.

Back at the house, Mrs. Price and Fiona were discussing the staff. "I am having trouble with Cecelia," admitted Fiona. "She will not follow my direction, and I am unsure what to do next."

"You must discipline her, Fiona. You must confirm your position as her superior, even if it means dismissing her for disobedience."

Fiona sighed. "I must try to think of a solution that

accomplishes what you say, but I do want to keep the peace if possible. Thank you, Mrs. Price. I will speak to her directly before it gets any worse."

Before Cecilia went to attend to Clara that evening, Fiona took her aside to speak with her. "Cecelia, you have not been performing the tasks that I have given you, and I must discipline you for your impertinent behavior. Beginning tomorrow, you will be suspended without pay for the remainder of the week. When your suspension is over, you may come back to work. If you continue with poor behavior, you will be dismissed completely. Do you have any questions?"

"Miss Clara is waiting for me to attend to her before dinner," said Cecelia haughtily as she turned on her heel and walked away. When she entered Clara's room, her sweet tone of voice returned. "Did you have a good day, Miss Clara?"

"Not that great," pouted Clara at her vanity table.

"I am sorry, Miss. Did something happen?" asked Cecelia.

Clara sighed. "I did not know that Abigail had come back to the house. She did not take the voyage with Nellie after all. She just makes things...complicated. That's all."

"She doesn't hold a candle to you, Miss Clara. You are beautiful and have such nice things now. What is more, you are from an important family. You are a Davenport," Cecelia said softly.

"I know. Mary is so fond of her, though. I wish that Mary looked at me the same way that she looks at Abigail. And I am Mary's own sister."

"I am sorry, Miss Clara. I have had a difficult day as well. Fiona continues to give me grief over my performance, even though I have worked my fingers to the bone these last years. I am afraid the power from her promotion has gone to her head. Did you—did you happen to ask Miss Mary today about Fiona's promotion, and if it may have been a misunderstanding?" Cecelia asked carefully.

"Oh, I am sorry. Even if I had remembered, I did not have the chance to speak with Mary. She went into town after breakfast, then asked Abigail to ride horses for the rest of the time. I am sorry that Fiona is giving you trouble though. It really does not seem her place. I will speak to Mary about it."

Cecelia thought for a moment, then made her move. "If I may say, Miss Clara, maybe you need a companion as much as Miss Mary does. Someone you can confide in, and who confides in you. Someone who does not complicate things, as you say. With your income from the estate now, you can certainly afford it."

"What would you know about my income anyway? My mother is managing my finances and I must clear it with her first. The idea of my own companion sounds enjoyable, but where would I find such a lady? I may have had a chance before with Nellie's introductions, but I am afraid the moment for that has long passed."

"Oh this hairstyle does look lovely on you, Miss Clara. There is no man alive who could resist you," said Cecelia as she smiled at her in the vanity mirror. "I think that it would be a privilege for any girl to be your companion. It could be the best thing that could ever happen for someone."

Clara smiled. "I am not so sure about that, but it is kind of you to say so. I suppose if I could find someone who would want to be…" she trailed off.

"I know that I would be overjoyed if a fine lady like you was to ask me to fill such a position," continued Cecelia as she delicately clasped the string of pearls around Clara's neck.

"Oh, I had not thought of that. You would want to be my companion, Cecelia? I wonder what Mary would think."

"You and I have been friends for years, Miss Clara. And do not forget that you are a Davenport as much as Miss Mary is. Abigail was her maid, and Miss Mary made her a companion. You can do anything that Miss Mary can, if it is what you wish."

Clara sat thoughtfully. "You are right. Perhaps it is time I began making my own decisions. Why don't you come see me tomorrow after breakfast and we will speak about it then. Mary may just have to find another housemaid to replace you."

"Oh, Miss Clara, you are the most generous person I know. Thank you so very much," Cecelia rambled excitedly. With Clara on her side, she would have certainty of her position at Davenport House—and there was nothing that Fiona or anyone else could do about it.

CHAPTER 11

Fiona scrambled to have everything in place the next morning. Without Cecelia working, Fiona would have to take care of much of the cleaning and attending the girls herself. Bridget was also working hard to keep Davenport House immaculate. Fiona thought that even when Cecelia returned from her suspension, the house could still use another maid. The girls were going to come down to breakfast at any moment. Fiona was tidying the drawing room when Mary walked in.

"Good morning, Miss Mary," said Fiona, trying not to sound too flustered.

"Good morning, Fiona. You look like you have been busy. Are you enjoying your new role here?"

"I am, Miss Mary. We are short a maid today, so I will be filling in as needed. I will attend you and Miss Clara," said Fiona.

"Very well. Is Cecelia ill?" asked Mary.

"No, Miss Mary. She…um…I am afraid that I had to suspend her from her duties this week. It was a disciplinary measure," explained Fiona.

"Oh, I see. I did not figure that the transition would go well with her. See to it that she is dismissed if she gives you any more trouble. I will ask Mrs. Price to be on the lookout for a new maid since you are working double duty."

"Thank you, Miss Mary," said Fiona. She was relieved that Mary seemed to understand.

Abigail went to visit the Valentis after breakfast with a knapsack full of goods from the kitchen. The children were delighted to see her. Phillip invited Abigail to take a walk with him to see the fruit trees that he had been working on.

"I met the Davenport sisters the other day," said Phillip as they walked through the grass with the children following behind. "They were kind enough to invite me to dinner. The food was delicious, so you can imagine my joy when I saw you approach the house with a knapsack from your kitchen."

"I am glad that you can use it, Phillip. The children must miss their mother's cooking," Abigail said. When she saw Phillip look to the ground in response, she hoped she did not make a mistake by mentioning his wife. "I am sorry, I should not have said that."

"You may say whatever you like, Miss Abigail. I just miss her. We all do," said Phillip sadly.

"Of course you do. She must have been a lovely lady to have raised such lovely children," Abigail said compassionately. She changed the subject so that Phillip would not feel he needed to speak of his wife if he did not wish to. "How long did you live in Pittsburgh?"

"My family came to America from Italy, and we settled in Pittsburgh when I was a boy. If I am honest, I will say that I am glad you will not be going on that ship. The trip across the ocean was difficult for us and certainly unsafe at times. Once my family heard of the ocean liner hitting that ice a few years back, I have been sure that I would never board one again."

"That is understandable. I was afraid to board the ship myself, and relieved that I did not have to go through with it after all," Abigail said. She could feel herself beginning to get emotional about that day and took a deep breath. "What did you do in Pittsburgh?"

"I started to work in the coal mines when I was fourteen. It was dangerous work, and once I married Sofia, she would pray every day that I would come home alive. But it was she who—" he stopped. "She started coughing real bad. The doctors said that it was consumption. I knew that I could not keep working in the mines and leave the children without a father too. After Sofia passed, I sold everything we had and moved us out here where I might have a chance to see my children grow. I have read about how to grow a garden and how to farm. I hope to be good at it someday." Abigail looked at Phillip for a moment. He was a strong man with a sturdy build about him. Abigail had no doubt that he would do well as a farmer.

Mary was in the upstairs sitting room when Fiona walked in. "Dr. Hamilton here to see you, Miss Mary."

Mary's heartbeat quickened when she heard his name. "Please show him in, Fiona," she said, trying to keep her composure.

William soon entered the room with his usual friendly smile. Without thinking, Mary stood up and hugged him. "What a nice way to be greeted by you," he whispered as he hugged her back.

She giggled. "I am sorry. It was automatic when you walked in. I suppose I am just very happy to see you."

"I am not sorry at all," said William with a smile. "How are you, Mary?"

"I am very well. I did not expect to see you for a long while."

"I can only stay a few minutes, but I have come to tell you some news of mine. And I have come to thank you."

"Thank me?" asked Mary in surprise.

"You have saved me. When you came into the office and told me of trying to do everything yourself and then making changes to the house staff, I realized that I was doing the very same. I admitted that I needed help, and that is when I got this letter. One of my grants has been approved! This means that I will have the funds to pay for the clinic to be staffed. A nurse can help the patients with everyday issues, and I will be there for when a doctor's training is required. I was so glad to see the letter that I came straight here to tell you."

"I am very happy for you, William! Does this mean that we may see you at the house more often?"

"I hope very much that is what it means. I will have to make inquiries to find qualified candidates, but I expect it will not be long before the clinic is staffed in the daytime. I can make house calls during the day, and then if I am fortunate enough to be invited for dinner at Davenport House again…" he trailed off and smiled at Mary.

"You are always invited. Every day. Thank you for coming to share your good news with me this morning," Mary said smiling. She was surprised how William seemed to bring out her honest feelings whenever he was near. She felt like she could tell him anything.

Mary walked him to his car in front of the house. They saw Abigail walking from the direction of the Valentis' just then. "Abigail!" called William, smiling as he waved to her.

Abigail tried to force a smile as she approached. "It is nice to see you, William," she greeted, seeming distracted.

"Are you feeling alright?" he asked concerned. She looked pale and anxious.

"I think I am alright. I only need to lie down for a bit I think. Please excuse me," said Abigail as she went into the house.

"Mary, please tell me. Is Abigail upset with me?" asked William sincerely.

"I don't think so. Why would she be?"

"I meant about stopping her at the pier in New York. I would understand if she was sore at me about it. She looked upset when she saw me just now. I wondered if it was because of what I did. I will feel badly of course if my worries come to nothing and I kept her from an opportunity."

"On the contrary, I was under the impression that she was grateful for your services. If she is upset about it, she has not said so to me," said Mary.

"I suppose that is a relief. I must be leaving now. I am glad to have seen you today, and perhaps I may come for dinner later this week," said William as he climbed into the driver's seat.

"I look forward to it," said Mary with a smile. She watched him drive away, wishing that she could be in the seat next to him.

"You wanted to see me after breakfast, Miss Clara?" said Cecelia obediently as she entered Clara's bedroom.

"Oh yes, come in. I have not had time to talk to my mother about your position. I will need her help to decide on a contract and a way to pay your allowance. For now, we will say your position as companion to me is a trial while we figure out the details. Is this agreeable to you?"

"Yes, Miss Clara. I am so happy that we will be able to speak as friends once more!"

Clara giggled. "Alright then. Why don't you change into something suitable and meet me for tea in the upstairs sitting room?"

"Right away, Miss Clara," Cecelia said excitedly, and ran out of the room. She nearly crashed into Fiona in the upstairs hallway as she ran to the stairs.

Fiona was surprised to see her. "Cecelia, what are you doing up here? You should be in the servants' quarters for the remainder of your suspension."

Cecelia laughed heartily. "I do not answer to you anymore. I am now a lady's companion to Miss Clara. It is you who will be following *my* orders. Now, go ready tea in the upstairs sitting room for Miss Clara and me." Cecelia laughed again as she ran to the stairs. Fiona stood in bewilderment.

"Are you certain that is what she said?" asked Mrs. Price.

Fiona nodded in distress. "I told her she would be suspended last night, and she now says that she is Miss Clara's own lady's companion."

"I do not want that flibbertigibbet around my daughter," said Mrs. Price honestly. "I will speak to Clara about this myself. She would not have known what a trouble

Cecelia has been as of late. Do not be discouraged, Fiona. I had already made inquiries for a new housemaid before any of this happened. I will follow through on the replies and see if we may get you more help."

Mary went to Abigail's room and knocked on the door. "Abigail? It is me, Mary."

Abigail opened the door. "Mary, I am sorry I left so suddenly. I was feeling dizzy and worried that I would faint."

"Oh dear, then you are ill. Should I call for William to come back?" asked Mary.

"You needn't bother him. I think I am just overwhelmed with feelings, not sickness. It has been a difficult week."

"Of course. William was worried that you were upset with him for keeping you from your trip with Nellie."

"That is another thing making me feel ill, Mary. When I was about to board the ship, I had a terrible feeling of dread. Like something bad would happen if I took another step. So now I fear for Nellie that something will happen to her," Abigail said as tears filled her eyes.

"Dear Abigail," Mary said as she embraced her friend. "We must try not to worry. I know it is difficult. I am glad that you are safe here with me for now."

"I do not expect you will need me so much when you marry William," said Abigail suddenly.

"Why would you say such a thing? We are not even engaged," Mary said blushing.

"I only wonder if I should think of a future for myself when I am no longer needed here."

"You must do as you see fit with your future," Mary answered. "I would never hold you back from having a life of your own, if that is what you wish."

Cecelia arrived in the upstairs sitting room, wearing her plain brown frock to wait for Clara. Fiona was setting tea on the table just then. "The fire needs to be stirred," giggled Cecelia when Fiona tried to walk out of the room. Fiona glanced at the fireplace and could see that the fire was going well, so she left quietly. "And tell the cook I will dine with the family now," Cecelia called loudly after her.

Clara was looking through the clothes in her room when her mother entered and closed the door behind her. "Please tell me it isn't true, that you have asked Cecelia to be your companion," Mrs. Price said worriedly.

"And what if it is true?" replied Clara defensively. "Mary is not the only Davenport who makes decisions in this house."

"Cecelia has been on thin ice downstairs ever since the sinister role she played with the former Mistress. Miss Mary or Abigail could very well have died because of what Cecelia did. Have you thought of that? Cecelia was disciplined just last night for her impertinence. She should not even be in this house, let alone upstairs with you," Mrs. Price urged.

Clara sat for a moment feeling ashamed. She was not aware of these things about Cecelia. Clara did not want to be taken for a fool, but also wished to save face in front of her mother. "If I say Cecelia will be my companion, then she will be. I am weary of others making decisions that should be mine and ordering how my life should be run. I am twenty-five-years-old and was given the chance of a life-time to see London with Nellie Whitmore. I could have even been married from there to a wealthy duke. You forced me to stay behind. Cecelia was my only friend downstairs for many years. I will not be held back by you any longer." Clara left the room to meet Cecelia in the sitting room for tea.

The laborers returned to the estate to continue construction on the unfinished sections of the stable. Ethan put the horses out in the pasture to be away from the noise. He hoped that Abigail would come out to ride Amethyst today. He looked toward the house. To his dismay, Clara and Cecelia seemed to be making their way toward him. He groaned and looked around quickly for a place to hide but it was too late.

"Ethan!" squealed Cecelia as she waved at him. He reluctantly walked in the direction of the girls and met them across the fence.

"Good morning, Ethan. I wanted to tell you the news. I have asked Cecelia to be my companion," said Clara proudly from the other side of the fence. Ethan nodded in response. "I also thought that perhaps you could teach me to ride today," said Clara, smiling and looking into his eyes.

"I thought you did not like horses," Ethan muttered.

"Well, I suppose I am more the type to like horses pulling my carriage, but I think today is a good day for me to learn to ride horseback."

"The laborers are working on the stable now, and all of the equipment is in there, so…" Ethan trailed off.

"Why Ethan! If I did not know any better, I would think you did not want to teach me to ride at all," Clara pouted.

"Come now, Ethan. Clara said she wants a riding lesson. She is your superior after all," Cecelia said with a smirk.

"Son?" called John Smith from across the pasture.

"I have to go," Ethan said to the girls. He ran as fast as he could to the other end of the pasture. "What is it, Pa?"

John Smith laughed. "I don't need you, Son. I just thought you might need me," he replied, nodding toward the girls by by the fence.

Ethan chuckled and shook his head. "You are more clever than anyone gives you credit. It is good to hear you laugh again. You seem happier than you have been in a while. Although I suppose I would be happy too, if I got to kiss a pretty girl like you did," Ethan remarked wryly.

John Smith smiled to remember it, then he grew serious. "You should not keep her waiting, Son. Girls like her are hard to find. I should know. I only found one my whole life and she made me happy for as long as she was alive. I am happy today because I know my son might have the same, if he can get to her before another fellow does."

Abigail was still pale and acting quiet when she went into the dining room with Mary for lunch. "An extra place has been set at the table," remarked Mary, feeling hopeful. "Have you heard if William is coming to lunch?"

"I have not heard," answered Abigail as she sat down. John Smith and Ethan filed in, followed by Clara and Cecelia. Mary and Abigail were confused to see Cecelia.

"Good afternoon, Mary," said Cecelia as she sat down at the extra place setting. "Have you heard from William today?"

Mary sat silently with her mouth open. She could not understand why Cecelia was there addressing her in a familiar way, or why Cecelia was there at all.

Clara spoke up. "Oh Mary, I meant to tell you. Cecelia is my companion now. You will need to find another housemaid." Cecelia looked up from her plate and smiled. She had finished her food before Clara finished her sentence.

Mary was still speechless. She looked at Mrs. Price who was serving their drinks at the table. Mrs. Price returned Mary's look helplessly. What followed was the longest awkward silence that anyone at Davenport House had known. Much to everyone's dismay, Cecelia attempted to rectify the silence with inane chatter throughout the meal. Ethan tried to meet eyes with Abigail, but she would only look at her plate.

. After lunch, Cecelia followed Clara up the grand staircase. "Clara, I wonder if I might choose my upstairs room now. I know that Richard's old room has been closed off while he has been away, but it does have such a splendid view of the gardens."

"You embarrassed me in there!" Clara snapped. "I am trying to prove to my mother and to Mary that I can make smart decisions. Now I have been made to look a fool. You will not have a room upstairs until you conduct yourself like a proper lady's companion!" Clara stormed into her room and closed the door, leaving Cecelia whimpering in the hallway.

Mary asked Mrs. Price and Fiona to meet her in the drawing room after lunch. "I was led to understand that Cecelia was being disciplined. How is it that she now expects to dine with us and live as Clara's companion?"

"I am sorry, Miss Mary. I have only just heard of it this morning," said Fiona anxiously. "I cannot fathom how she persuaded Miss Clara to arrange such a thing."

"I tried to talk sense into my daughter when I discovered the change, but she insists that she makes her own decisions," said Mrs. Price sorrowfully.

Mary sighed. "Clara is right. She must be allowed to establish her place and make her own decisions. It would not be right to restrict her from the friends she may choose. I know what it is like to be restricted in my own home, and I would not wish that feeling on Clara. Although I do not know why she would choose Cecelia. I am not sure I can endure another meal such as that one. However, we simply must get used to this change as best we can so that Clara may feel at home here."

Mary knocked on Abigail's bedroom door after speaking with Fiona and Mrs. Price. "Abigail, would you like to go for a ride with me? I certainly need one after that dreadful meal today."

"Thank you, Mary, but I am still feeling a little weak. Please go on ahead without me."

"You have not been eating," remarked Mary. "Should I send for William?"

"You need not send for him," answered Abigail. "He has been so very busy with people who need him more than I."

"He did tell me that he will have more time to spare now, as he will take on a nurse to run the clinic," Mary said smiling.

"I am happy for you, Mary. I am sure we will see more of him if that is the case. Please do not worry for me. When my appetite returns, I am sure I will feel better. In the meantime, would you be able to see to it that the Valentis receive the food?"

Mary smiled and held Abigail's hand. "You are always thinking of others. I will ask Bridget to ensure the Valentis receive the food. Have a good rest, Abigail."

Mary arrived at the stable and asked Ethan to ready Dolly for her. "Right away, Miss Mary. Should I also saddle Amethyst? For Abigail?"

"Abigail declined to ride today," answered Mary.

"She is not ill, is she?" Ethan asked quickly in concern.

"She did not eat any of her lunch."

Mary looked at him carefully. "You have grown to care for her, haven't you?"

Ethan could feel his face turning red and he looked down. "I want to know that she is alright. I thought that I might die when she went to board that ship in New York. That morning when I spoke to you harshly…it was because I was upset with myself for not telling her how much I care."

Mary hugged Ethan and kissed his cheek. "She is fortunate to have your affections. I am glad you brought her back to us. Will you ride over the fields with me this afternoon?"

"Of course, Miss Mary."

It was nearly time to change for dinner. Cecelia nervously entered Clara's bedroom on her best behavior. "Good evening, Clara. What will you be wearing to dinner tonight?"

"I believe that I will wear my yellow gown and string of pearls. They do look darling together," answered Clara smiling. She loved to talk about her new clothes.

"Yes, it is a charming combination, to be sure. Only, I am afraid that I do not have anything to wear to dinner. All I have is this plain frock."

"You must have savings that you can use for a new dress," Clara said while looking through her jewelry.

"Sadly, I do not have any savings. I thought perhaps you had something I might borrow. Just for tonight, of course," said Cecelia quietly.

Clara looked up and laughed in disbelief. "You could not possibly fit into any of my dresses. Your waist is wider and you are half my height. Even if my dresses did fit you, I would never consent to it. Do you know how expensive these gowns are, and how much I have had to endure just to have nice things? You can purchase your own clothes when you receive your allowance."

"I see," said Cecelia disappointed. "And when might I expect to receive an allowance?"

Clara huffed impatiently. "I have not spoken to my mother about it yet. Just go to dinner wearing what you already have, before I change my mind about this whole arrangement."

Abigail was lying in bed when Cecelia burst through her bedroom door. "I need to borrow a dress for dinner tonight," she said urgently.

"Oh, I am sorry Cecelia. I have nothing to lend you," Abigail answered wearily.

"But I must have something. What about all those new dresses you have been wearing since you returned from New York? Surely you can spare one and alter it for me," Cecelia persisted.

"It is simply not possible, Cecelia. If you bring me some fabric and sewing supplies, I can do my best to make something nice for you," Abigail offered.

"I do not have any fabric, and I need something tonight," whined Cecelia. "Why does everyone in this house get new things except for me? Even Fiona has a new dress, and she is only the housekeeper. I am a lady's companion and I have nothing!"

"Perhaps you can ask Clara about it," Abigail suggested.

"Well thank you for nothing," Cecelia huffed as she left the room and slammed the door behind her.

Mary and Ethan headed back with their horses barely in time to change for dinner. "You see, Ethan," Mary said seriously. "I am afraid to admit that I am also in love."

Ethan nodded. "I know, Miss Mary."

Mary blushed. "It is obvious, isn't it? I do not know what comes over me, but I seem to blurt out whatever is on my mind when he is near. When he came to visit, I ran and hugged him without even thinking!"

"I am sure he did not mind one bit," smiled Ethan. "He did ask about you on our drive to Philadelphia."

Mary gasped. "Did he truly? And what did you tell him?"

Ethan smiled. "I told him that I was protective of you and that if he wanted you he must go through me first."

Mary laughed. "Well do not scare him off. I am only afraid that he does not feel as much for me as I feel for him. He may only think of me as a friend."

"You can ask him at dinner tonight," laughed Ethan. "I hear his car coming up the drive now."

"Dr. Hamilton to see you in the drawing room, Miss Mary," announced Fiona when Mary came into the house. Mary was still in her riding clothes, but eager to meet him.

"William, good evening!" she cried. "Have you come for dinner?"

"I certainly have," he answered with a smile. "If it is still alright, that is. I am sorry I could not give proper notice. Although I am now pleased to announce that the Yorktown clinic has a nurse on staff."

"It is wonderful news," said Mary. "I must go to my room to change now, but please tell me all about it at dinner."

Much to everyone's relief, Cecelia was not at the dinner table that night. Abigail still looked pale, but tried to eat and even smile while William told everyone of the news from Yorktown. He spoke plenty about the clinic's new nurse, and how honored he was to begin working with her every day. Mary tried to remain calm as William continued to praise the perfectly qualified Nurse Roberts. Ethan looked at Abigail intently but she would not look back at him.

After dinner, Mary and William went into the drawing room for tea. Clara went back to her room, and Abigail and Ethan were left alone in the dining room. "Are you feeling alright? I am worried for you," said Ethan.

Abigail nodded but still did not look at him. "I am not very hungry."

"Maybe a ride with Amethyst will help you feel better," offered Ethan. Abigail shook her head and stood up from her chair to leave. "Have I done or said something wrong? I am worried that you have avoided me, but I do not know why. There are things I would like to speak with you about."

"I must speak with you too," said Abigail. "Perhaps I will go to the stable to see Amethyst tonight, but I am not fit to ride."

Ethan nodded. "I will walk with you," he offered. Abigail and Ethan were unaware that they were being watched from a window of the house when they went to the stable together that night.

Abigail looked fondly at Amethyst. "Sometimes I imagine that she actually is happy to see me," she said.

"Of course she is. Abigail, my stomach is twisting in knots waiting for what you have to say to me," said Ethan worriedly.

Abigail faced Ethan and looked into his eyes. "Phillip Valenti has asked me to marry him."

Ethan held his breath. He was not expecting anything like this. "How did you answer him?" Ethan whispered.

Abigail looked down. "I have not answered him. I was so surprised when he asked that I could not speak. I said that I would visit him later with a reply."

"I see. Do you love him?" asked Ethan bluntly.

Abigail shook her head. "I love his children. But I wonder if Phillip does not so much wish for a wife as he does a mother for Gabriella and Donnie."

"You should give him your reply and not keep him in suspense," said Ethan.

Abigail nodded. "What is it you wished to speak to me about?"

Ethan looked very tired all of a sudden. Abigail's revelation had caught him off-guard and he was not sure how to proceed. "There is something I have wanted to say to you for a long time. Do you remember when you asked me if I was engaged?"

Abigail nodded. "Of course. I have not been able to forget it."

"I have wanted to tell you that my engagement was called off not long after you asked. Only, I have not known how to tell you."

"When was this?" asked Abigail surprised.

"It was weeks ago," answered Ethan.

"Are you certain that it was over between you weeks ago?" Abigail asked sadly as she looked down.

"What do you mean?"

"I saw Clara come to your room upstairs...you were

whispering together in the doorway. Then the whispering stopped and I heard your door close. It was the night I went outside and Phillip came to me for help with the children."

Ethan hung his head in shame. "I did not know that you saw us that night. Yet I lectured you the next day and you did not even mention it. Clara came to my room that night and I told her to leave. I did not want to see her. I closed the door and she left. Then I went outside for the night air. I wanted to speak with you when I saw you but... you left with him."

"What do you think I should tell him?" asked Abigail suddenly.

"You must do what will make you happy. You deserve to be happy. I cannot tell you what I think no matter how much I may want to. The decision is yours alone."

Clara still watched the stable from her window as Cecelia entered her room. "How was your dinner, Clara?" she asked.

"It was fine," Clara answered, still staring out the window. Cecelia walked over to see what she was looking at.

"Is that Abigail coming out of the stable?" asked Cecelia.

Clara nodded. "She went in a while ago with Ethan but never went riding. Now she appears to be returning to the house alone."

Cecelia shook her head. "She does like to visit the men at night, doesn't she?"

"What men? What do you mean?" Clara questioned.

"Have you forgotten that while you and I were still maids, we could see everything that happened in this house—and the family was none the wiser," answered Cecelia mysteriously.

"What do you know?" demanded Clara.

"Well, I happen to know something about Abigail that Mary would certainly not like to hear about her own companion. Mary may even dismiss her for it. Ethan would likely never speak to her again…if he only knew," replied Cecelia sensationally.

"Just say it, Cecelia! You are wearing on my nerves," cried Clara impatiently.

Cecelia sighed. "It is really not my place to gossip. I would not want to cause trouble. Oh I do wish that I only had a dress suitable for dinner…" she rambled.

"Oh for Heaven's sake, I will buy you a dress! Now tell me what you know!"

Cecelia smiled. "Abigail spent the night…with the neighbor, Mr. Valenti! Then she sneaked in through the servants' entrance the next morning so that Mary would not see her."

Clara was skeptical. "Are you certain about this?" she asked. Cecelia slowly nodded and smiled.

CHAPTER 12

Clara and Cecelia took the carriage to Yorktown directly after breakfast the next day. Abigail was feeling better after eating that morning and went with Mary for a morning ride. "Nellie should be almost to Liverpool by now," mentioned Abigail. "I do hope we hear from her soon."

"I am certain that we will. I am sorry that you did not get to see London with her. Perhaps I can take you to Philadelphia again, or even New York."

"It is kind of you to offer Mary, but you needn't make a special trip only for me," Abigail replied. "I have grown to love my home here and I am quite content to stay."

"I am glad to hear you say it. I think that after Clara returns with the carriage, I would like to visit William at the clinic. Do you wish to accompany me? He will be glad to see that you are feeling better."

"Wouldn't you rather speak to him alone?" asked Abigail with a smile. "I will go if you wish me to, but I did promise to call on the Valentis today."

"In that case, you should keep your promise. I will go see

William alone. If only it were proper for ladies to be the ones to propose marriage to men. Men take far too long about expressing their intentions."

Abigail laughed. "I see that your visit to town will be very eventful indeed. I will be sorry to miss it."

Mary and Abigail were in the upstairs sitting room having tea when Clara returned with the carriage. Clara met them in the sitting room, and Cecelia soon followed wearing a yellow ruffled dress trimmed in black with a scoop neckline. Mary tried to be friendly. "Good afternoon, Cecelia. I will ask Fiona to bring more teacups."

"Don't bother, Mary. I have already told her," said Cecelia as she strutted through the room.

"I will leave for town in a few moments to see how the clinic is coming along," Mary remarked. "William will have more free time now that there is a nurse on staff."

"Isn't that romantic? I wonder what she looks like," rambled Cecelia. "Clara told me that Nurse Roberts is all that William could talk about last night. She is fortunate to spend all day with a handsome doctor...and all night," Cecelia laughed. Mary looked aghast at the suggestion.

Clara spoke up. "Oh hush, Cecelia, you are bothering Mary. We all know that William loves her. Have the two of you become engaged yet, Mary?" she asked bluntly.

"I—I am not engaged. If I was, I surely would have announced it," Mary said bewildered.

Clara shrugged. "I thought that you may have been secretly engaged. I have been secretly engaged before."

The room fell silent. Mary was astonished at Clara's revelation, however she felt relieved that the spotlight was off of herself for a moment. "You have been engaged, Clara?" Mary asked, thinking she cannot have heard her right.

"I was engaged to Ethan for two years," Clara said casually. "I had to break it off though. Now that I am one of the family, I can do far better than a stable boy."

Cecelia was giggling, but Mary and Abigail were in stunned silence that Clara could make such a remark. "Oh, do not look at me that way, Mary. If you want to know about secret engagements, you should talk to Abigail," said Clara. Cecelia could hardly contain her glee at the scandalous conversation unfolding before her.

"Me?" cried Abigail. "I do not know what you mean."

"Don't you?" asked Clara. "Do you mean to say that you are not engaged to Phillip Valenti?" The room was silent again as everyone looked at Abigail's horrified face.

"I am not engaged to him," Abigail replied, her voice shaking.

"We thought you must have been," said Cecelia. "Since you stayed all night at his house and came in secretly through the servants' quarters the next morning."

"You must be mistaken, Cecelia. Abigail would not have done such a thing," Mary said to defend her.

"Is Cecelia mistaken, Abigail? Or did you spend the night at our neighbor's house?" asked Clara, watching Mary's face carefully.

"I can explain," said Abigail flustered. "I was not with Phillip. I was only helping the children and I accidentally fell asleep on their bed."

Cecelia giggled. "Of course you did, Abigail. No one would suspect otherwise." The room was quiet again.

"I must get ready to go into town," Mary whispered. She stood up and walked out of the room.

"Perhaps you would have been better off going with Nellie," Clara said to Abigail, then she and Cecelia laughed together.

Abigail got up quickly and followed Mary to her room. "Oh Mary, please say that you believe me," she said anxiously. "I was so tired that day, and I did not realize that I had fallen asleep until sunrise."

Mary closed the door so that she and Abigail could speak privately. "I do believe you. Only, I do not know what to do about Clara. She and Cecelia are out of control. I am even worried to attend meals in my own home because of what they might blurt out. Thank goodness that Cecelia has not been able to say anything to William yet. The way that she talked about him spending all day with the new nurse...oh Abigail, I am suddenly frightened that William might never want me."

"He loves you, Mary. Perhaps he is only waiting until your mourning is complete to say something," Abigail offered.

Mary's face lit up. "Oh! That must be it! Thank you Abigail!" Mary hugged her tightly. "I did not even think of it. William is only being a proper gentleman, waiting to express his intentions because I am in mourning. It makes perfect sense!"

Abigail smiled. "I am sure that is the reason. No one could dispute his intentions when they see how he looks at you."

Mary sighed deeply in relief and sat upon her bed. "You have just taken a thousand worries off my shoulders. I am sorry that the girls were cruel to you just now. I know you do not deserve it."

"It would have been better if I had just told you about when I fell asleep at the Valentis' myself. I certainly did not wish for you to hear it the way they said it. You have been honest with me about your feelings for William, and I should be honest with you also. The truth is, Phillip did ask me to marry him."

Mary gasped. "Have you answered him?"

"I intended to answer him today after you left for Yorktown," replied Abigail shyly.

"What will you say to him?" asked Mary anxiously. "You do not have to tell me if you do not wish to."

"I do wish to tell you. I usually guard my feelings so strictly, but I already feel as though a weight has lifted by telling you this much. I believe that Phillip may be attracted to me, but he seems more eager to have me as a mother to his children, than as a wife for himself. I do get along with the children so well," Abigail said as she smiled. "But I cannot marry him for this reason alone. That is what I will tell him today."

It was a sunny afternoon in Yorktown when Mary walked into the open door of the clinic. "Mary," William greeted cheerfully when she walked in. "How good of you to visit. You are just in time to meet Nurse Roberts. She is just finishing up with a patient now." Mary could hear muffled conversation behind one of the room dividers.

Mary held her breath. "Very well," she said hesitantly.

"Nurse Roberts is the best thing to happen to this clinic. She was nursing in the days of the Great Rebellion," William said proudly.

"The War of the Rebellion?" whispered Mary astonished.

"But that was fifty years ago!" Just then, a woman who looked elderly yet tough emerged from behind the room divider.

William made introductions. "Nurse Roberts, this is Miss Mary Davenport—the first friend I made when I moved here."

Nurse Roberts nodded stoically at Mary. "It is time for my lunch break, Doctor," she said. Nurse Roberts slowly walked out the door of the clinic.

Mary stifled a giggle. "Oh William, I was so afraid to meet her!"

William laughed heartily. "Well she scares me a little too, but why would you be afraid to meet her?"

Mary sighed and looked down when she felt her face turning red. "I was just worried that the new nurse would be prettier than me."

William gently lifted Mary's chin so that he could look into her eyes. "Impossible," he said.

Abigail returned from the Valentis' house just in time to change for dinner. Phillip was disappointed but understanding when Abigail told him she must decline his proposal. He said that she would still be welcome at any time. Abigail thoughtfully went up to her bedroom and looked through her wardrobe for the dress she would wear to dinner that night.

Ethan was brushing the horses when he heard footsteps coming toward the stable. He hoped that it was Abigail. "Good evening," said Clara's voice. She was wearing her best gown and jewelry that night. "I am glad that I found you before you went into the house for dinner."

"What is it, Clara?" asked Ethan without looking up.

"Won't you even look at me?" she pouted. He continued

brushing the horses. "I learned a secret about Abigail…don't you want to hear? She will be leaving Davenport House."

Ethan looked up. "What do you mean? When?"

Clara shrugged mysteriously. "Mary found out that Abigail spent the night at the neighbor's house. I don't see how Mary can keep a girl with such questionable morals as her companion. Mary must think of the Davenport name, you know. Perhaps Abigail will marry Phillip to salvage what is left of her reputation. Still, she will not be fit to be associated with us."

"I already know about Abigail going to the Valentis' that night. And I will defend her to you, or to Mary, or to anyone else who might question it! Abigail is an *honorable* woman, Clara. Something that you know nothing about!" Ethan stormed out of the stable, leaving Clara alone in bewilderment.

Mrs. Price and Fiona were conversing in the servants' lobby when Abigail burst in looking pale and frightened. "What is it, Miss Abigail?" asked Fiona, becoming concerned.

"One of my dresses is missing!" she cried.

"Perhaps it has only been misplaced or has gone to the laundry. I will ask Bridget," said Fiona, trying to calm Abigail.

"But—Cecelia wanted one of my dresses and was angry when I did not give her one. I am afraid that she has taken it!"

"We will check her room," Mrs. Price said abruptly. Abigail followed Mrs. Price and Fiona to Cecelia's room. There, crumpled in a heap on the floor, was the dress that Abigail was missing. She began to cry as she went to the dress and gingerly lifted it up. Some of the seams were ripped open and the skirt was torn as if someone too large for it had tried to wear it anyway.

"I am so sorry, Miss Abigail!" Fiona apologized. "We will mend it immediately."

"No," said Abigail with tears running down her cheeks. She carefully draped the dress over her arm and stood up to leave. "I will take care of it myself. I will need to borrow the sewing kit."

Mary had dressed for dinner and went to Abigail's bedroom to see if she was ready. She heard crying from inside the room. "Abigail?" Mary asked as she slowly opened the door. Abigail was sitting on the floor with tearful eyes. "Dear Abigail. Did things end badly with Phillip?"

Abigail shook her head. "I am not upset about Phillip. I am upset about this," she said, carefully holding up the dress. "It belonged to Ethan's mother. Cecelia has stolen it from my wardrobe and torn it."

Mary gasped. "This dress belonged to Ethan's mother? How did it get here?"

"When I came back to Davenport House without my luggage, Ethan and his father gave me her dresses to wear."

Mary could feel tears stinging her eyes as she carefully lifted the skirt and ran her hand across it. "I thought that your new clothes looked familiar, but I was so young when she was still with us. I thought I was only imagining things."

"I promised them that I would take care of her dresses, and now look," Abigail cried sorrowfully.

"Oh, Abigail…Ethan must love you very much to give these to you. I am sure that he will understand. I will see to it that Cecelia leaves this house once and for all." Mary stepped out of the room just in time to see Ethan knocking on her bedroom door. "Ethan, I am over here," Mary told him from the hallway.

He walked toward her. "Miss Mary, Abigail did not do anything wrong that night at the Valentis'—"

"I know she didn't," Mary interrupted.

"Then you will not dismiss her?" asked Ethan.

"No, I would never! She is my best friend in the world. Why would you have the idea that I could dismiss her?"

Ethan looked hesitant to answer. Mary shook her head. "It does not matter now. What matters is, Abigail needs you." Mary led Ethan down the hallway to Abigail's room.

"What has happened?" Ethan asked Abigail as he knelt to the floor to sit beside her. Mary quietly left the room while Abigail explained everything about the dress.

"Are you terribly upset with me?" Abigail asked him nervously.

Ethan put his arms around her and whispered, "I know you did everything you could. I would never blame you for this."

"I have something to tell you," Abigail whispered back. "I declined Phillip's proposal today." Ethan held her closer to him, and neither of them said anything for a long while.

Clara was alone in her bedroom when Cecelia entered gleefully wearing her new yellow dress. "Did our plan work?" she asked.

"No. It was a disaster," Clara scowled. "Now he hates me more than ever."

Cecelia was disappointed. "Oh well, we can try something else."

"*We* are not going to try anything. I have changed my mind about having you for my companion. I want you to go back downstairs and we will forget that this ever happened," Clara said firmly.

"But Clara—I'm sorry—please—I—I—" Cecelia sobbed and ranted. "Let me talk to Ethan. I will fix it for you! Abigail is not even a real lady! She is only a hotel maid pretending to be one!"

"Don't you ever dare say anything to Ethan!" Clara shouted at her. "And if I ever hear you speak of Abigail in that way again, I will see to it that you are dismissed without a reference!" Clara stormed out of her room and hurried down the hallway, trying to take deep breaths before she went to dinner. Mary met her on the upstairs landing.

"Clara, there is something I must speak to you about. It is Cecelia. She has done something dreadful," Mary began.

"You don't need to tell me. Cecelia is no longer my companion. I have sent her back downstairs. It was a mistake that I asked her in the first place." Clara could feel tears stinging her eyes as she recalled the shameful events from the past week. "Oh Mary, I have made so many mistakes. Can you forgive me?"

Mary smiled and hugged her sister. "Of course I forgive you. Dinner is nearly ready now. Let us go down together."

Mary and Clara were the only ones in the dining room that night. They chatted happily about the future of the estate and other possibilities in managing their income. Mary even decided to have a ride after dinner. She felt happier than she had in a long time as she thought about the wonderful things to come. The new stable would be complete soon. William might come visit her more often. Mrs. Price was finding new housemaids to make up for the shortage in staff. The future seemed bright for Davenport House.

CHAPTER 13

It was early on a Saturday morning when Fiona answered the front door of Davenport House. "Dr. Hamilton!" she greeted in surprise. "Please, come in out of the rain. Miss Mary is still in her room. Should I tell her that you wish to see her now?"

Dr. Hamilton's expression was very grave. "Yes. I am afraid it is urgent." Fiona led him to the upstairs sitting room and went to tell Mary.

Mary tried to wake, but she was confused. "William is here to see me now?" she asked again.

"Yes, Miss Mary. He said it is urgent. He waits for you in the upstairs sitting room."

"Thank you, Fiona. Please tell him that I will meet him as soon as I get dressed."

"Very good, Miss Mary," answered Fiona.

Mary dressed quickly and did not take the time to put her hair up. She went to the sitting room to see William there, looking downcast, and holding a newspaper in his arm. "What is it?" she asked worriedly.

"It is very bad, Mary. You must sit down," he answered.

Mary obeyed and grew more anxious by the second. William continued sadly, "Yesterday, the ship that Nellie was on, the Lusitania…it was sunk by the Germans. Over half of the people aboard are now presumed to be dead."

Mary gasped and covered her heart with her hands. "I cannot believe it. Let me see!" She took the newspaper and read the headline over and over. "It can't be. It simply can't be!"

"I am very sorry. I came directly here when I saw it."

"But there are survivors, aren't there? Nellie could be one of the survivors!" cried Mary hopefully.

"She could be," William said as he put his arm around her.

Mary became angry. "But how could those awful Germans do such a thing! Who would kill so many innocent people traveling across the ocean?"

"That is the other thing, Mary. Americans have died on the ship. This means that our president may have no choice but to declare our country at war."

"I hope he does declare war! I hope we kill every horrid German on that continent!" Mary sobbed emotionally.

William swallowed the lump in his throat. "I think that I should leave you now. This newspaper can stay here for anyone else who needs to see it." He got up to leave while Mary cried on the settee, covering her face with her hands.

"William! Wait!" Ethan called from the top of the staircase just before William went out the front door. Ethan hurried down the stairs. "What has happened?"

"Perhaps we should speak outside," suggested William. "Find your pa, too. He should hear what I have to say."

Abigail and Clara dressed quickly and left their rooms

when they heard the voices in the house. Fiona explained to them that Dr. Hamilton had just been in to see Mary with urgent news. They found Mary in the sitting room appearing inconsolable, but William was gone. "What has happened, Mary?" asked Clara worriedly. Mary showed them the newspaper.

"Oh no!" whispered Abigail as she read the headline. "William was right." She sat next to Mary and put her arm around her.

Clara gasped in horror. "Mary—I am so sorry!"

Mrs. Price entered the room worriedly. Clara held up the newspaper for her to see. Her mother gasped, then saw Mary still inconsolable on the settee. "What can I do to help her?" Mrs. Price asked Abigail.

"You should order that her meals be sent to her room," Abigail said calmly. "Have a meeting with the staff and tell them what has happened. We do not yet know who may have had loved ones on that ship, or whether we will be at war tomorrow."

Mary finished crying after a while and appeared to stare blankly in front of her. She would not respond when the girls talked to her. Clara looked at Abigail helplessly. "Let us help her to her room," Abigail said quietly to Clara. "We should make sure that she has tea available. She has done a fair bit of crying." Clara nodded and they helped Mary walk back to her room and get into bed. Mary continued to stare blankly and did not appear to be aware that Clara and Abigail were even there helping her. When Mary fell asleep, the girls quietly left the room.

Clara turned to Abigail in the hallway with wide eyes. "Abigail, I have done something truly wicked. I do not know if even God can forgive me for nearly being a murderer. I wanted Nellie to take you away from the house. I wanted you to go on that ship," Clara confessed with tears in her eyes.

"You will do better in the future, Clara. I am certain of it," Abigail said kindly. Then she grew very serious. "Mary has taken the news today very hard, and I am afraid that she will sink further into depression unless we learn that Nellie has lived. You must speak with your mother and help her to run the house as long as Mary stays in her room. I will stay with Mary today until she wakes."

Clara nodded, then looked down at the floor. "I am sorry for what I have done to you. You never deserved it and I am ashamed. If there is anything I can do..."

"You can take care of the Valentis while I attend to Mary. They are so poor and weary. It would mean the world to them to know that we have not forgotten our neighbors," Abigail explained. Clara nodded and walked away.

The new housemaids arrived and Fiona showed them to Cecelia's old bedroom which they would share. Fiona also instructed her sister Bridget to attend to Mary and Clara while she was busy with training the new housemaids.

Clara went to the servants' quarters to speak with Fiona. "Please ensure that Mary and Abigail receive their meals in Mary's room, and that hot tea is available to them at all times."

"Very good, Miss Clara," answered Fiona.

"Is there anything that I may take to the Valentis today?" asked Clara.

"Your aunt has set aside some things for them in the kitchen."

"Thank you, Fiona. It is likely that Mary will remain in her room for the coming days, so please come to me with any questions or concerns. I do not wish for her to be disturbed."

"Very good, Miss Clara."

William had spoken to Ethan and John Smith for a long while on the front steps of the house before he finally shook their hands and drove away in the rain. Ethan and his father walked to the stable with much to think about. "Do you think we will be made to fight, Pa?" asked Ethan.

"War hurts a lot of people, Son. I hope we never see the day. My pa and all of his brothers were killed in the War of the Rebellion. It left my ma and her sisters without husbands. It's a terrible thing for the women."

Ethan nodded. "I understand." Ethan went to care for the horses and his father returned to the house.

"Ethan?" called Clara's voice from inside the stable. She stood there holding a basket with fresh goods from the kitchen.

Ethan sighed. "If that is for me, it won't do you any good."

"No, I am taking it to the Valentis. I wanted to speak with you first."

"Now is not the time, Clara."

"I am ashamed for the way I spoke to you last night… the things that I said about Abigail. You were right to defend her. And now I must forever live with the guilt from nearly sending an innocent girl to her death. I know that you love her. I will not stand in your way again and perhaps someday you will forgive me. I am going to work closely with Mother now to run the estate and find my place in life. You need not worry about me coming to you anymore." She turned to leave.

"Thank you," Ethan said quietly as Clara walked away from the stable for the last time.

CHAPTER 14

Mrs. Price continued to oversee the completion of the stable over the next several days. The new housemaids settled in, and Clara took on new responsibilities while learning about business from her mother. Mary remained in her room and Abigail continued to attend to her. Ethan was in the stable retrieving the carriage horses for Clara's ride into Yorktown.

"Ethan?" called Abigail wearily. He ran to her when he heard her voice and put his arms around her.

"Are you alright? I have been worried for you," Ethan said quietly.

"I am only tired, but it is Mary who we should worry for. She does not seem to improve. I did not realize how shaken she would be from the news of the other day. I nearly went on the ship myself, and although I ache for all of those poor families, I find myself otherwise recovered."

"I am glad you feel recovered. I have missed you," Ethan said.

"I had forgotten what the new stable looks like. It is nearly finished now," Abigail smiled. "But there is something I would like to know your thoughts about. Do you remember that feeling I told you that I had, when I nearly boarded the ship that day? Whenever I think of Nellie now, I do not have that terrible feeling. Surely if she had drowned then I would know it in my heart. I think that she may be one of the survivors. Do you believe that a person can feel such things?" Abigail asked hopefully.

Ethan smiled at her. "I do," he said.

"Thank you for saving my life that day," she blushed.

"Thank you for coming back with me. I don't know how I could have lived without you," Ethan said sincerely.

Abigail returned to the house to check on Mary. Clara anxiously ran to meet Abigail in the Hall. "A telegram has just arrived for Mary. It is from London!" she cried. "Do you think that we should take it to her or—should we read it first before she sees it?"

Abigail thought for a moment. "Let us see what it says. If it is bad news, we may need to withhold it while she remains in this condition."

Clara nodded. She opened the telegram and they read it together.

MISS MARY DAVENPORT

DAVENPORT HOUSE, YORK COUNTY, PENNSYLVANIA

MY NIECE HAS ARRIVED UNHARMED BY THE GERMAN SAVAGES [STOP] SHE WILL REMAIN AT MY LONDON RESIDENCE UNTIL FURTHER NOTICE [STOP]

LUCINDA WHITMORE

Clara sighed in relief. "Oh, thank goodness. Poor

Nellie must have been through so much to get to safety. I cannot imagine the horror!"

"I will take this to Mary now!" Abigail hurried up the stairs. "Mary, a telegram has arrived for you," she said smiling as she sat on the edge of Mary's bed.

Mary took it from her and read it slowly. Then she sighed and handed the telegram back to Abigail.

"This is good news," Abigail said gently, wondering if Mary had truly understood what she read. "Nellie has arrived safely in London."

Mary nodded. "I am glad. I must try to sleep. I am so very tired."

"You have not eaten your breakfast or lunch. You must eat something to keep your strength. Please," begged Abigail. Mary did not seem to hear. She turned on her side and closed her eyes as if going to sleep.

Abigail left Mary's room sadly. Clara was waiting outside. "What did she say? She must be so happy."

Abigail shook her head. "She is not in her right mind. She scarcely reacted at all when she read the telegram."

"I am just leaving for Yorktown now. Is there anything that I may bring back for her?" asked Clara thoughtfully.

"Take me with you. It is time to ask William to come to the house," said Abigail seriously.

Abigail walked into the clinic in Yorktown while Clara went to the shop next door. William was surprised to see her, and suddenly became worried. "Is it Mary? Did she hear bad news of Nellie?" he asked nervously.

"We have just received word that Nellie arrived safely to her aunt's house," Abigail started. "But when Mary found out, she hardly reacted. She has stayed in her room ever since hearing the news of that dreadful day. She will hardly eat or speak to anyone."

William sighed. "I am afraid that Mary is regressing. It has not been long since the tragedy with her father. When Mary heard the news of the ship, it must have brought back the trauma and grievous feelings. She has tried to be strong in running the estate alone and going on as if nothing had ever happened. Unfortunately, it could only last for so long before it caught up with her."

Abigail nodded. "I understand now. I suppose I had forgotten about all of that terrible business. So much seems to have happened since then."

"You are right, and that is likely a reason she is feeling this way now. It was all too much. Mary needs you more than ever. You must persuade her to eat and drink," said William.

"Won't you come to the house, William? To see her yourself?" asked Abigail.

"I do not think there is anything I can do for her," he replied sadly. "She needs food and water and time to heal."

"I do not mean to come see Mary as a doctor, but as a friend who cares for her," said Abigail gently.

"I do not think that Mary wants to see me," he said quietly.

"Why would you think that? I imagine that she may want to see you more than anyone," said Abigail.

"I wish that was the case, but I do not want to intrude," he said.

Abigail took his hand and looked into his eyes. "You have saved my life more than once. I know that it is you who will save Mary, too. Please, come to the house to see her," she implored him.

William could not refuse her gentle eyes and selfless plea. There was also something about the way that Abigail looked today in the beautiful dress she wore that made William feel sentimental and like he would do anything for her. "I will come to the house," he agreed.

Abigail returned to the carriage where Clara was waiting. "He is going to see Mary now," said Abigail. "Did you buy what you needed?"

"I did," smiled Clara. She showed Abigail an adorable little doll wearing a ruffled dress. "It is for Gabriella."

Abigail gasped. "Oh, she will be delighted! How thoughtful of you, Clara."

"I have purchased a toy for Donnie as well. Those poor children have nothing. I know it is not much, but I do hope it might make their lives a little brighter."

"Of course it will," said Abigail sincerely, climbing into the carriage.

Fiona met Dr. Hamilton at the front door and showed him to Mary's room. He saw that Mary was awake in her bed staring blankly at a full dinner tray that lay next to her.

"Mary?" he said as he walked over to her.

Mary seemed surprised to see him and sat up in bed. "Dr. Hamilton…is someone at the house ill? Do you have more news?"

"No," he replied. "I have come to visit you as a friend, if you'll have me."

"Did you hear that Nellie has survived?" she asked quietly.

"I did. I was glad to hear the news of her. But it is not the thought of Nellie that has made you feel this way, is it?" he asked carefully.

Mary shook her head and tears filled her eyes. "I miss

my father...and I do not understand how my own family could have been so terrible to me," her voice cracked and she began to weep uncontrollably, harder than she ever had before. William held Mary close and allowed her tears to fall on his shoulder. He stayed with her for a long while.

Clara and Abigail were waiting in suspense outside of Mary's room. William finally emerged from the room holding a tray of cleared off dishes. He smiled when he saw the girls waiting there. "She is asking for more dinner," he said with a laugh.

"I will get it!" exclaimed Clara as she took the tray from him and hurried down the stairs.

"How is she?" asked Abigail.

"She had a good cry, which may have been what she needed," answered William.

Abigail smiled at him. "Yes, I am sure that is what she needed. Thank you for coming."

"It was my pleasure," he replied with a smile. "Only, may I make a request? Is there any chance I could have some of that delicious smelling dinner for myself? I am starved all of a sudden."

Abigail giggled. "I will tell our cook."

CHAPTER 15

Clara and Abigail were pleased to see Mary arrive at breakfast the next morning. Mary finished her food quickly and was embarrassed to ask for more.

"You have not eaten in days," remarked Abigail with a smile. "You must make up for it now."

Mary giggled. "I must be careful or I may become too heavy to ride Dolly. She would not like it. Abigail, what do you say to going for a ride after breakfast?"

Abigail smiled. "It sounds wonderful. Would you like to come, Clara?"

"You two go ahead. I told the Valentis that I would visit them before lunch. Mr. Valenti has the most interesting stories about Pittsburgh. It has become very modernized, apparently. I have some things that I would like to take to the children as well."

"I am happy that our neighbors have not felt neglected these past days. Well done, Clara," said Mary.

Clara beamed. "There is more good news for you, Mary. The apartment above the stable was furnished this morning for Ethan and his father."

"Oh, that is good news! Poor Ethan has been trapped here with all us girls. He will be relieved, I am certain," replied Mary.

Ethan was happy to see Mary looking so well as she and Abigail approached the stable. "Good morning, Miss Mary," he said smiling.

"I have heard that your apartment is complete. Perhaps you may show Abigail and me before we take our ride today," suggested Mary.

"Yes, of course." He led them up the staircase in the back and showed them the new rooms and kitchen. He turned the lights on to show that they were electric. "Pa is still scared of using the lights," Ethan remarked. "But I expect he will get used to it."

"This is delightful," said Abigail. "Mrs. Price has furnished it nicely. Will you be happy here, even though it is quite different from your loft before?"

"I expect to be very happy here," he answered. "Pa and I will be set up to sleep here tonight."

"I will miss you at the house, but I know that this is where you want to be anyway," said Mary. "Let us go down for our ride now. I have been aching to take Dolly out again."

Mrs. Price and Clara were in the library when Mary walked in after her ride. "Oh, good afternoon. I did not think that anyone was in here," said Mary.

"The accounts are ready for your review at any time," said Clara proudly.

Mary looked through the ledger. "You have been busy! I am pleased that you have taken an interest in the estate. There are many possibilities with five hundred acres."

"Mother has been helping me with the finances and Phillip has given some ideas on development. He tells me of how advanced the city has become in only five years," Clara chatted excitedly.

"Wonderful. How did you meet Phillip? Is he one of the laborers?" asked Mary.

"No," laughed Clara. "Phillip Valenti…our neighbor."

"Oh goodness, I had forgotten his name for a moment. You seem to be very happy though, Clara. I do believe this is the happiest I have seen you," mentioned Mary.

"She is discovering her purpose as a Davenport," Mrs. Price said proudly.

Ethan and John Smith were settling in at the apartment above the stable. "Well Son, I suppose we are back to potatoes and carrot stew again," said John Smith disappointed.

Ethan laughed. "I suppose that in the end, living in that grand house wasn't so bad after all."

John Smith raised his eyebrow. "Have you talked to your young lady yet?"

Ethan shook his head. "I haven't, Pa."

"I told you to be quick before some other fellow asks her," said his father.

Ethan sighed. "I am ashamed to admit that another fellow already did ask her. Thank goodness she declined him."

"Didn't I tell you, Son? You better hurry, or another fellow is going to ask her before you get to it."

"I have wanted to," Ethan said wearily. "But every time I have tried to say something, the words won't come out."

John Smith chuckled. "I was the same way with your ma. She was already promised to another fellow when I finally got to asking her."

"She can't have been," said Ethan in disbelief. "I never would have thought that you could do such a thing. The other fellow must have been terribly disappointed."

John Smith continued to chuckle. "There is a lot you don't know about that time. I expect the fellow was disappointed, but only because it meant he would not get the family money. Maryanne was a proper lady, you know. I was only the gardener. She gave up her whole life to be with me. And I did whatever I could to make her happy," he said with tears forming in his eyes. "It made us happy to see each other happy. We didn't need the family money for that."

Ethan was stunned. His father had never told him any of this before. "How did you finally ask her?" he questioned.

"Well, it was like you said. Every time I tried, the words would not come out. So I found a way to ask her without needing to say much. Wait here a moment, Son."

Bridget attended to Mary in her room while Clara was there talking to her. Abigail knocked at the door and entered the room. "Mary, William has come for dinner tonight," Abigail announced. She smiled at Mary's surprised expression, then left the room to change for dinner.

"Oh my goodness," said Mary. "The last time he was here, I was a crying mess. Please make me look pretty tonight, Bridget. Oh dear, I am suddenly nervous. At least Ethan and his father will be at dinner tonight. Wait! They might think that they must not dine with us anymore since they have moved out of the house. Clara, please go tell Ethan and John Smith that we wish to still dine with them tonight and every night. Oh, my face is still swollen from yesterday," rambled Mary as she looked in the mirror. Clara left the room and closed the door behind her. She stood in the hallway for a moment trying to think about what she should do.

Abigail had just dressed for dinner and was about to open her door when someone knocked on the other side. "Clara," said Abigail in surprise. "I am going down to dinner now."

"Well, that's the thing," Clara began nervously. "Mary has just asked me to tell Ethan and his pa that they are invited to dine with us every night even though they have moved from the house. I wonder if you could tell them instead of me. They will be happy to see you."

Abigail smiled. "Of course I will. I am sure they will be pleased to hear it."

Abigail went up the stairs to the apartment above the stable and knocked on the door. Ethan came to the door, but his eyes grew wide when he saw that it was Abigail. He closed the door behind him quickly and met with her on the landing. "Good evening," he said.

"I am sorry if I startled you," said Abigail. Ethan seemed to be acting jumpy.

"Oh, it is nothing," he said nervously. "Are you on your way to dinner?"

"Yes, and I have come with a message from Mary. You and your father are invited to dine with us tonight and every night," she said with a smile. "She needs you especially tonight because William is coming to dinner and Mary feels nervous."

The door to the apartment opened abruptly and John Smith hurried out and closed the door behind him. "What are we waiting for, Son? Let's go eat."

Mary entered the drawing room where William and

Clara were waiting. William smiled when he saw her. "I am glad to see you feeling better, Mary. I hope it is alright that I came for dinner tonight."

"The invitation is always open. I am glad to see you. Thank you for visiting yesterday," Mary replied. Abigail walked in with Ethan and John Smith. They all went into the dining room as everyone was eager to begin their meal.

"Has President Wilson decided if we are going to be at war?" Mary asked William.

"He has not. Although, many including myself were certain that he would after the Lusitania was hit. There is much tension right now between the the people who want war and those who do not," replied William.

"It's a good thing he has not declared war," said John Smith. Everyone at the table was surprised to hear him speak. "War is like a plague. It killed most of my family. It is not what I would ever wish for my son and his family."

"I do hope the War is over before we need to worry about sending our men from here," William said seriously. "Oh, I am sorry if I have spoken of things I shouldn't have at dinner. Forgive me, Mary."

"It was I who asked you, William," replied Mary. "But perhaps you may answer another question I have for you. Do you suppose that your clinic will be having a telephone installed?"

"I expect I must, eventually. I do not know who would phone me," William laughed. "Does anyone in Yorktown have a telephone?"

"You may be surprised, William," said Clara. "Phillip tells me that he was in the room when his employer phoned

San Francisco from Pittsburgh. The whole country is connected now."

"Well, I must consider it more seriously then," said William. "Thank you, Clara."

"We will be having a telephone installed soon," announced Mary proudly. "I have recently decided it…although Nellie Whitmore is the only person I know who has a telephone, and she is away in London. If you get a telephone, William, I will phone you so that you will not feel left out."

William laughed and smiled at Mary. "Very well, you have convinced me. The clinic will have a telephone this year and will eagerly await it's first ring from Davenport House."

Chapter 16

The next morning at breakfast, the girls were discussing how well the new housemaids seemed to be adjusting. "I am impressed with Fiona especially," said Mary. "She has exceeded my expectations in training the maids. Did you know that Fiona is only sixteen?"

"She does a lovely job, Mary," agreed Abigail. "I understand that she is the pride of her family. The Miller's have nine children with not a son among them."

"Phillip was fortunate to have a daughter and a son," giggled Clara. "That reminds me, Mary. Would you have any objection to my showing the Valenti children the house today? They have wished to see it very much, as they only got to see the kitchen the one time they were here. Phillip must go into town and I offered to care for the children in the afternoon."

"Oh Clara, that is a wonderful idea. Of course you must show them the house," said Mary with a smile. "I will be discussing the telephone installation with Mrs. Price today. Do you have any plans, Abigail?"

"I did not make plans, but if you will be occupied here then I think that I may go for a ride," she answered.

Abigail changed into riding clothes and walked down the hallway for the stairs. She had just reached the upstairs landing when she could hear the sound of children's laughter coming from the other hallway. She smiled as she went to Clara's room and knocked on the door.

"Miss Abigail!" Gabriella exclaimed as she swung open Clara's door. "How do you like my new dress and my string of pearls?" Abigail was surprised to find Gabriella wearing one of Clara's new dresses with Clara's pearl necklace.

"You are a fine lady," answered Abigail. Gabriella picked up her dress and carried it with her as she strutted around the room.

Clara was sitting at her vanity table giggling while Donnie sat in her lap, happily brushing his own hair with Clara's soft hairbrush. "Good afternoon, Abigail," Clara smiled. "We are just about to have a tour of the family rooms downstairs. I have told the children about the conservatory and they do not believe me that there are plants living inside of a house."

"I am pleased to see the children again, and looking so well. Have a lovely time with your tour," Abigail said as she left the room and closed the door behind her. She was looking forward to seeing Ethan and did not want to keep him waiting for her.

When Abigail was nearly to the staircase, she heard the front door open and Fiona's voice announced a visitor. "Miss Mary, the chief of police is here to see you."

Abigail's heart sank and a feeling of dread filled her stomach. She immediately went back to Clara's room and opened the door to speak with her. "Clara, now is not a good time to take the children downstairs. You should keep them here in your room for as long as you can," she said seriously. Clara nodded in agreement, even though she did not understand Abigail's reason. Abigail closed the door and went downstairs.

"I am sorry to come here like this Mary, but there are things you need to know," Chief Reynolds began, meeting with Mary in the drawing room.

"Have you made progress on the case?" Mary could feel her stomach twisting as she remembered the family scandal that killed her father and nearly killed her only weeks ago.

"The first thing I will tell you is that you should prepare yourself for the likelihood of your mother being released," Chief Reynolds said solemnly.

"I do not understand. Is not there more than enough evidence against her?" asked Mary in dismay.

"While we do have the confession of your brother and the evidence of poisoning, it is only circumstantial. At first, your mother was obstinate when we attempted to question her. Instead of speaking with us, she demanded a public apology, claiming that her arrest was unlawful. She must have grown weary of waiting for her friends to come to her rescue, because she is now talking to us and giving us a different story. She claims that one of the housemaids was the true conspirator. We were not sure what to think of your mother's claims that your brother Richard and this housemaid were secretly a couple. Your mother claims that it was the maid who schemed to ensure that Richard would receive an inheritance. Yesterday, we received word that this maid arrived at the jail in Johnstown to visit Richard, which offers corroboration to your mother's story."

"Cecelia?" Mary asked incredulous. Abigail and Mrs. Price were now standing in the doorway and heard every word that the chief had told Mary.

Chief Reynolds nodded. "I must ask that you send for the police immediately the next time you see her."

Mary shuddered. "She was dismissed from her position here not two weeks ago, and no one has seen her since."

Mrs. Price was alarmed. "Who could have thought the silly girl was as conniving as that?" she thought aloud. "To think that she was so close to my own daughter! Oh heavens…" Mrs. Price said as she sat down on a chair before her knees gave out from under her.

"I am in shock at this news of Cecelia, Chief Reynolds. But you have also said that my mother might be released, and that frightens me. She must hate me now more than ever," said Mary.

"Your mother has powerful friends who have insisted on your mother's innocence every day since her arrest. She could be released any day now, unless we find another reason to detain her," warned the chief.

Mary looked at him helplessly. "Will she come back here?" she asked.

"You know your mother better than I do," said Chief Reynolds. "You should prepare yourself either way."

After Chief Reynolds left the house, Clara came downstairs with the children. "What was that about? Is it safe to come out with the children now?" she asked.

"Yes," Abigail told her, trying to manage a smile.

"The children may see the rest of the house now. We will explain later."

Clara walked the children back to their house at the end of the afternoon. When she returned, Mrs. Price, Mary, and Abigail were waiting for her. They explained to her what the chief had told them.

"I am so sorry, Mary. Cecelia did not seem clever enough to be involved in anything so sinister. I was ashamed of my decision to have her as my companion already," said Clara.

"We did not tell you this information to shame you, Clara. You only must be aware that Cecelia is wanted by the police. It is also possible that my mother may try to return to the house if she is released from jail," Mary said solemnly.

"Heaven forbid. She may hate you, Mary, but it cannot be as violently as she hates me!" cried Clara.

"And me," added Mrs. Price quietly. It felt like a dark cloud hung over the drawing room.

Just before dinner that night, Ethan waited for Abigail to come down the grand staircase so he could speak with her privately. "Abigail," he said from the bottom of the staircase. "I was waiting at the stable with Amethyst for you all afternoon. Did you change your mind about riding today?"

Abigail cringed. "Oh dear! I am very sorry, Ethan. I must have forgotten about riding when Chief Reynolds came to the house. I feel terrible that I kept you waiting."

"What did the chief have to say?" questioned Ethan.

"Perhaps it is better if Mary tells you herself," said Abigail worriedly. "It was not the news that any of us wanted to hear."

"Do you think that you will ride after dinner tonight?" he asked her hopefully.

Abigail tried to smile. "I do not know when I will be riding again. Mary needs me now. If she chooses to ride then I will go with her, but I cannot abandon her during this time."

Ethan nodded. "I understand. Don't forget that Amethyst misses you terribly," he said quietly.

Mary came down the stairs and saw Ethan. "I must tell you our news," she said to him. "Let us speak in the library before we go in to dinner."

"I am sorry, Miss Mary," Ethan said grimly after Mary explained to him the police chief's visit. "What will we do if your mother comes back to the house?"

"That is what we are trying to decide. I was able to stand up to her once before, but I feel so weak now. I do not know how I will find the strength to do it again," Mary answered, looking defeated.

Ethan looked into her eyes. "You must, Miss Mary. I know you fear her, but this may be the most important thing you ever do. You cannot let her take over the house again or it will hurt everyone in it."

They all walked into the dining room solemnly. Mary was disappointed that William did not come for dinner. She desperately wanted to speak with him that night.

Abigail stayed close to Mary over the next several days. Mary tried to act as though things were normal, but everyone in the house knew better. Mrs. Price thought it best to warn the servants about what might be coming. Clara felt relieved that she could escape the tension and anxiety in the house by visiting the Valentis often. Mary wrote to

William every day renewing the invitation for dinner, but he did not write back or come to visit.

It was raining hard one afternoon when Ethan saw Mary running into the stable in distress. "William does not love me," she cried to him.

"What do you mean? I cannot believe it," Ethan said.

"He will not answer my letters or visit the house! He has forgotten about me," she cried.

"I do not think that is possible. It must be something else," said Ethan.

Mary wiped the tears from her eyes. "Have you asked Abigail yet?" she questioned.

Ethan shook his head. "I just don't feel like I can," he said. "My last engagement was a disaster. Every time I see Clara, I am frightened that it might end the same way. Maybe Abigail deserves a man better than me anyway. She might find someone who can give her a proper house."

"You must face your fears, just as you have said that I should. Abigail has already received an offer of marriage," said Mary seriously.

Ethan held his breath and felt as if his heart stopped. "What? Who?"

"Phillip Valenti," answered Mary.

Ethan heaved a sigh of relief. "Dear God, Mary. You nearly scared me to death just now! I already know about Phillip Valenti. Abigail told me that she refused him."

"She told you about refusing him, and you did not ask her there and then?" Mary scolded.

Ethan turned red. "I know, I am just so scared."

"I suppose I do not have the right to scold. I am scared as well. Oh Ethan," she sighed. "If William will not have me, and Abigail will not have you, then you and I will always have each other—right?"

Ethan hugged Mary and kissed her forehead. "I will always be here, but you should not give up on William just yet. Let us take the carriage into Yorktown and you can talk to him at the clinic."

"But, it is raining," Mary said.

Ethan smiled. "It is only a sprinkle."

Ethan and Mary arrived in Yorktown in the rain. Ethan found shelter under the awning of a shop, and Mary walked through the muddy street to reach the door of the clinic. The "OPEN" sign had been taken down and it seemed dark through the window. Mary knocked on the door. She tried the handle but it was locked. She walked back toward Ethan. The pouring rain splattered on the rooftops loudly around them. Mary was becoming drenched from her hat down to the heels of her boots. "William is not here!" she shouted to Ethan through the rain.

Ethan nodded toward the clinic and shouted back, "He must be! His horse and car are just there!" Ethan started to feel bad for taking Mary out in this weather.

Mary turned to look at the clinic behind her just in time to see William briefly open the door, then close it abruptly. Mary looked to Ethan in dismay while the rain poured down on her.

"He must not have seen you!" Ethan shouted, although he knew it was not true. "Try knocking on the door again!"

Mary returned to the door of the clinic. "William?" she called as she knocked.

William opened the door quickly and let her in, then

closed the door behind her. "Mary," he said. "You should not be out in this rain." He handed her clean linens to dry with.

"I needed to see you. Why have you not come to the house or answered my letters? I am afraid I must have done something to offend you. I am sorry for what I said before about the War. I was upset and I did not mean it," Mary rambled as she tried to dry off and fix her hair.

"It is nothing you have done, Mary. But I do not think that I can visit you anymore, and you should not try to visit me either," William said seriously.

"What do you mean? I must have done something terrible if you no longer want to see me," Mary said, feeling tears forming.

"I am closing the clinic. I must move back to Philadelphia," William answered sadly.

Mary sat quietly in shock. "I will die if you leave," she said bluntly.

William pulled a chair up next to Mary and put his arm around her. "I feel like I might, too," he said.

She turned and looked into his sad eyes, which were welling with tears. "Then why are you leaving?"

"Someone is threatening me. I am afraid of what might happen if I stay, or if I continue to see you at the house," William answered. He got up from his chair and went to the desk. He took a key from his pocket and used it to open the bottom desk drawer. "I returned to the clinic after house calls just days ago and found this note on my desk," he said holding up a paper. "Nurse Roberts was here but said she did not see who left it." He gave it to Mary to read.

Wilhelm Herrmann,

A doctor who changes his name has something to hide. Leave Yorktown or the world will hear that you are a German spy.

Mary gasped. "Who could ever suggest such a thing?"

"I am at a loss, Mary. I was not even aware that I had an enemy. But tensions are high just now. Some people are very angry that we are not fighting in the War. The newspapers say that children in Germany were given a holiday from school to celebrate the Lusitania being hit. It is a bad time to be a German in America, or anywhere else."

"It must be someone who knew you before you came to Yorktown. How else would they know your real name?" asked Mary.

"I have not used that name since before I went to University. I cannot imagine who it could be, or why they would threaten me for living here. Mary if this accusation went public…it could be very bad for me and anyone I associate with. I have already let Nurse Roberts go so that she will not be caught up in it."

"But the threat is untrue! You have helped so many people here. They must know it is impossible for you to be a spy," Mary reasoned.

"Of course it is not true, but it is a dangerous rumor for me, and for you if I keep seeing you."

"But—" Mary protested emotionally. "I have missed you."

"I have missed you, Mary. I am sorry if I ever caused you to think that I did not care, or that I did not want to see you anymore because I stayed away. I wanted you to be safe from all of this."

"You have put so much work into this clinic. How terrible if it was all for nothing," Mary said sadly. "I do not want you to be in danger, but I do not know how I will go on without you. That is to say, the town cannot go on without you. We must have a doctor closer than Lancaster," Mary persisted.

"I wish things were different, but this is the world we live in," he said looking down. "Sometimes we cannot have the lives that we wish for."

"I have just had an idea!" cried Mary suddenly. "You must show this to Chief Reynolds. Perhaps he can find the person who is threatening you."

William sighed. "I did not even want to show it to you, let alone the chief of police. I cannot let word of this get out."

Mary's momentary hope turned into despair. "Then, there is no solution. You will leave and I will never see you again."

"I am sorry, Mary. Please go now, before I change my mind and put us all in danger," his voice cracked in anguish.

Mary stood up to leave and walked to the door. William was just about to open it for her when she took his hand and turned to face him. They looked at each other intently. "Would it be alright if I kissed you goodbye?" he asked. Mary nodded. William slowly leaned forward and kissed her softly. "Goodbye, Mary."

She could not speak. She went out the door and walked through the mud to the carriage. The rain was starting to let up and Ethan was waiting for her. "Miss Mary, what has happened?" he asked as he helped her into the carriage.

Tears were running down her face. "Take us home as quickly as possible."

They arrived at Davenport House, but Mary did not feel prepared to go in and face the others. She decided to walk around to the gardens to pick flowers for her father's grave. She planned to visit her father for a few moments before she retired to bed to cry for the rest of the day. As she walked past the woods to the family cemetery, she could feel her heart sinking into her stomach at the sight of what was ahead. A tall figure stood there at the grave, wearing a long black dress and a thick black veil.

Mary dropped the flowers that were in her hand and tried to turn and run, but she was frozen in place. The figure turned around to face her. "Good afternoon, Mary," said the voice of Mrs. Davenport from behind the veil.

Mary ran into the house. Fiona and Mrs. Price were in the Hall and Abigail was just coming down the staircase. "What is it?" asked Abigail concerned. Mrs. Price and Fiona watched Mary for the answer.

Mary answered in a frantic whisper. "Mother is here."

Just after Mary retreated to her bedroom, Mrs. Davenport walked casually through the front door of Davenport House, as if she had not been away in jail for the last month. "Mrs. Price, where are you?" she called from the Hall. "Come take my hat and gloves and hurry up about it."

Mrs. Price appeared from behind a marble column. "I am no longer the housekeeper here, Margaret," she said bravely.

"Well that is one thing that Mary has changed for the better. Perhaps I should give the girl more credit. Davenport House was in need of a new housekeeper for years," she sneered at Mrs. Price.

"I will take those for you, Madam," Fiona said nervously to Mrs. Davenport.

She turned to look Fiona up and down. "It is beyond me why Mary would hire a child to do the job, but it's an improvement nonetheless." Mrs. Davenport held her head up high and walked up the staircase to her old bedroom, as if nothing had changed at all.

Abigail went to visit Mary in her room. Mary lay upon her bed, crying. "I am sorry, Mary. I understand why you are upset. Perhaps jail has changed your mother and she will not be so bad now," Abigail suggested optimistically.

"I am not crying about Mother," Mary said between sobs. "William is leaving for Philadelphia and never coming back!"

Abigail quickly put her arms around Mary. "Oh, how terrible! I never would have dreamed it! Has anything happened to his family?"

Mary sighed. "Someone has discovered that he is from Germany and is threatening to spread horrid lies about him if he stays."

Abigail gasped. "How could anyone do such a wicked thing? I promise that I have never told a soul about him."

"I believe you, of course. In a single day, my life feels as though it has been ruined. Perhaps I should have asked William if I could leave to Philadelphia with him. Then I would be with him and away from this miserable house," cried Mary.

Abigail tried to smile. "You must do what you think is best. But Mary, are you prepared to give up your house and your life here?"

"With Mother's return, it does not feel like any kind of

a life or even my house. What can I do? She acts as if she intends to live here again."

"You must find out from her," said Abigail. "Perhaps she has only come to visit."

"I doubt that is the case. I will find out from her at dinner. I cannot leave all of you alone with her tonight."

Abigail sighed in relief. "Thank you, Mary. I was just about have dinner ordered to my room."

"I think it is unwise for us to run away from her, as we have in the past. She might take over the house and throw everyone out if we remain too fearful to challenger her. No Abigail, we must face her tonight—no matter what she says or does."

It was very tense in the drawing room where they met before dinner. "What is this, Mary?" demanded Mrs. Davenport. "I leave for four weeks and suddenly the servants are dining at our table? Have I not raised you better than this? Not to mention, you must be going bankrupt."

"The finances are doing very well. Thank you for asking, Mother," replied Mary, trying to appear confident. "Let us go in to dinner."

Everyone felt their nerves on edge at the dinner table. John Smith and Ethan were starting to wish they had opted for potato stew at the stable that night, while the others surmised that they were not so very hungry after all.

"I see you have built a new stable," remarked Mrs. Davenport. "It looks quite expensive. They are only horses, Mary. They do not need a palace."

"It was Father's wish to build a modern stable with electric lights and more room. I was continuing with his plan," Mary replied calmly.

"And how are the Valentis?" Mrs. Davenport asked. Clara dropped her fork on her plate. Mary and the others looked at each other.

"Have you met our new neighbors already, Mother?" asked Mary bewildered.

Mrs. Davenport laughed. "Goodness, no. I do not call on farmers. I suppose I must have heard it from someone in town. My friends keep me informed, you see, since my own daughter finds it too hard to write to me herself."

"If you'll excuse me, Miss Mary," interrupted John Smith. "I need to check how the seedlings held up in the rain."

"And I have to bring the horses in," added Ethan as he stood abruptly.

"Son, I'll help you," said John Smith, and the two of them hurried out of the room.

"Honestly, Mary. Those two will eat us out of house and home if you keep feeding them like this," said Mrs. Davenport.

"Won't you be staying in your cottage now, Mother?" asked Mary.

Mrs. Davenport grimaced. "That place is in deplorable condition. It will take months for it to be fit to live in. I will stay in my room here until it the necessary improvements are made."

Mary took a deep breath. "If you intend to stay in the house, then I must insist that you do not complain about the changes that I have made. My friends dine with us every night and I have already worked out the cost." Mrs. Davenport did not respond, and the rest of the meal was eaten in the oppressive silence that saturated the room.

Mary took a walk in the gardens after dinner to feel

the cool air on her hot face. Dinner was miserable, and Mary hoped that she had done everything possible to stand up to her mother. It at least made her forget her troubles with William for the time being. "Miss Mary," called John Smith's voice from the gardens behind her.

Mary turned around. "Good evening, Mr. Smith. I am sorry about dinner," Mary said, feeling embarrassed.

"I hope you don't think me ungrateful if I eat at my new home from now on," he said, not wanting to look her in the eye.

"I will leave the decision to you. Of course I will not think you ungrateful. Perhaps I will even join you myself," said Mary wryly as she managed a smile. Then she shook her head sadly. "I am fatigued by her incessant rude comments. She is merciless to everyone in the house and almost seems to enjoy our despair. I wonder how much longer I will be able to hold up with her staying here. She insists that her cottage is unfit. She could prolong her stay indefinitely." Mary shuddered.

"My boy is reading a book from your pa's library that might help you. He reads it to me sometimes, and it has advice for your problem," suggested John Smith.

Mary looked confused. "I was not aware of such a book. Do you know what it is called?" asked Mary curiously.

"Sorry, I do not know. You might ask him about it," he replied.

Mary returned to the house and sighed heavily when she could hear the sound of her mother yelling at the new housemaids for not having dusted the bedroom. Mary thought better of going upstairs, and turned around to head for the stable instead. She asked Ethan to saddle Dolly for her and he happily obliged, still looking a little sheepish for leaving the dinner early.

Mary galloped over the fields in the dark enjoying the feeling of the brisk air flowing through her hair and clothes. *Why can't being in my own house feel this happy and freeing? It certainly never will as long as Mother continues to belittle me and everyone else,* she thought.

When Mary returned from her ride and was about to go back into the house, Ethan handed her a book. "Pa said that you were asking about this one," he said.

Mary laughed when she read the title aloud. "*The Art of War.* Your pa must have been tricking me."

"Do you not wish to read it, then?" asked Ethan confused.

"Oh, I suppose I had better take it with me," Mary replied. "You saw what dinner was like."

Ethan chuckled. "Good luck with that, Miss Mary," he called after her as she walked away with the book in her arm.

CHAPTER 17

S everal days went by, and the tensions in the house did not improve. Clara, however, seemed to be more cheerful than everyone else. She met Abigail in the upstairs sitting room and closed the doors to speak to her in private. "I must tell someone my news, or I might burst," she said to Abigail. "Phillip Valenti has asked me to be his wife!"

"Oh my!" Abigail exclaimed in surprise. "How did you answer?"

"I said that I would like to," Clara blushed.

"How wonderful! The children must be pleased. But Clara, I must ask...are you only looking for an escape from this house, or do you truly wish to be married to Phillip? I know it has been unbearable here as of late," Abigail said carefully.

"I understand why you might ask that, but I do feel that I love him. He is so very strong and handsome. I cannot stop thinking about him," she giggled. "Although his farmhouse is modest in size, I sometimes feel at home when I am there with the children. Abigail, I am ashamed that I ever accused you of questionable conduct at his house. I can see now just how much time and energy it takes to be with the children. And I do love them dearly now. Most women my age have three or more children, so I suppose I needed a head start," she said with a smile.

"I am very happy for you. Phillip is a good man and I believe you will become a happy family together," said Abigail.

"Thank you for that. I have told Phillip everything about the family scandal and my past mistakes. He wishes to marry me despite those things. I don't think that I could expect the same from a man of a wealthy and important family. I believe we can be very happy. The only thing is, I want to ask Mary if I may invite Phillip to dinner so that we may announce our news, but I do not believe it to be wise while her mother is here," said Clara. "I have kept to my room every night for no other reason."

"I understand, of course. You must make your announcement when the time is right."

Mary slept late that day after spending the previous night finishing the book that Ethan sent with her. She did feel more confident than before, although her heart ached whenever she thought of dear William. Mary knew that she must be strong, and she determined within herself to not think of him until after she had dealt with her mother. Then, she would go to Philadelphia to find him if she had to, so she could tell him how much she really cared, hoping that he returned the feeling. She could not forget about the way he kissed her, so sadly yet tenderly. It was a kiss she could never forget and she hoped he would not forget it either.

Abigail went to the stable to see Ethan. "Should I ready Amethyst for you?" he asked.

"Yes, I would like that. And I am sorry to have kept you waiting that other day," she added.

Ethan smiled. "I am afraid that I am the one who has kept you waiting all this while," he said, his face turning red. "I cannot hold it against you for making me wait just the one time."

Abigail smiled, although she was not quite sure if he was saying what she thought she heard.

"Would it be alright if I accompanied you on your ride today?" he asked. "It seems a long while since we talked." Abigail agreed happily and they went riding until it was nearly time for dinner. When they returned to the stable to put the horses away, Ethan seemed nervous.

"What is it?" asked Abigail with a smile. She had enjoyed their afternoon together very much and could not think why Ethan seemed almost upset now.

"Abigail, I—I—" he stammered, then sighed heavily. "I have wanted to give you something, if you wish it to be yours."

"What is it?" she asked curiously.

"It is in the apartment upstairs. Would you come up with me?" he asked nervously.

"Oh," Abigail hesitated. "But would it be proper for me to see it alone with you?"

"Pa is there. It will be alright," he answered. They went up the steps to the apartment and Ethan asked her to wait on the landing. He went through the door and Abigail could hear him saying, "Pa, I have brought Abigail with me so I can show her now." Then Ethan came back out for her. "Pa said he will wait in the kitchen. I hope you like it. And if you don't like it, you don't have to say you do," he stammered.

"You have me in suspense," she giggled. "I cannot imagine what the surprise must be."

Ethan suddenly put his arms around her. "Please say you wish it to be yours," he whispered. He opened the door and led her through. Abigail gasped at what she saw elegantly draped over an ornate wooden chest.

"Oh, Ethan! It is beautiful! Was it your mother's?" Abigail whispered happily. Ethan nodded. "And you truly wish for me to have it?"

"I wish for you to have it more than anything," he said. "If you will have it. If you will have me."

Abigail smiled and took his hands in hers. She turned to look once more at the beautiful white wedding gown and veil that made the whole room glow. She whispered to Ethan, "Yes, I will have you."

Mary had just changed for dinner when she heard a familiar sound outside. She ran to Abigail's room to the window that overlooked the drive. William was driving up in his motor car. Mary put her hands over her heart. "William has not left yet," she whispered to herself. She tried to keep her composure and soon heard Fiona's voice behind her.

"Dr. Hamilton here to see you urgently," Fiona said. "He waits in the upstairs sitting room." Mary thought it must have been a stroke of luck that Fiona did not show him into the drawing room where the others were waiting.

"You are here," Mary said as she entered the sitting room. William quickly closed the doors behind them.

"I took your advice and showed the note to Chief Reynolds," said William. "Now we know who left it at the clinic."

"Oh I am so glad you found the terrible person. Does this mean that you will not be leaving? Can you have it resolved with the man who wrote it?" Mary rambled.

"Mary, if you will just give me a chance to tell you. Chief Reynolds recognized the handwriting and compared it to his records. It was a perfect match—to your mother's writing."

Mary gasped, then became angry. "Oh, I should have known! She must have had her friends spy on you and look into your past. I am so angry!"

"But Mary, will she make good on this threat? I have to know," asked William anxiously.

"Not if I have anything to do with it! You will stay for dinner tonight, and then my mother will need to explain to her friends why she was seen associating with a German spy. She will not let it get out if you dine with her," Mary assured him.

"Are you certain about this, Mary?" he asked.

"She cares about nothing more than saving face in front of her friends. Leave it to me," she said confidently. "Please, come downstairs to have dinner with us."

When William entered the drawing room, Mary expected the tension to increase. But Ethan, Abigail, John Smith, and even Clara looked quite cheerful considering that Mrs. Davenport was there sulking in the room.

"Mother," Mary said confidently to Mrs. Davenport who sat across from her. "Dr. Hamilton will be dining with us tonight."

Mrs. Davenport turned her head in disgust and looked away from Mary and William. "I do not dine with German savages," she proclaimed loudly. The room fell silent and mouths hung open. The others were not sure that the words they just heard were possible for even Mrs. Davenport to have uttered. They began to think up excuses that would allow them to leave the room immediately.

Mary felt a rush of anger washing over her. "Now look here!" Mary said so loudly and suddenly that it made everyone in the room jump. "I have tried to be civil with you, but you will not listen. You continue to berate me and everyone around me. You have shown me that to be heard by you I must speak to you in threats, which is the only language you understand! If you *ever* insult my friends again, or if I hear even the slightest gossip in town that is slanderous to Dr. Hamilton, I will go to Henrietta Prichard, and Mabel Lewis, and everyone you know! I will tell them all about how I found the old town doctor—who is now in jail for covering up Father's murder—in *your* bed, when Father had not been buried a week!"

Silence fell over the room once more. Everyone sat in shock, but no one was shocked more than Mrs. Davenport, who trembled before Mary as if she was looking at a ghost. Knowing that this was one scandal she could not recover from, Mrs. Davenport stood up and hurried out of the room.

"Mary! That was positively wicked!" exclaimed Abigail.

Mary was unapologetic. "Dr. Hamilton might have been injured because of my mother's lies. At the very least, her threats would have left our town without the medical attention we need, all because of her infatuation with the last doctor. I do not take these or her many other offenses lightly."

"You must have liked the book," Ethan remarked, trying to hide his smile.

"Thank goodness you said something to her, Mary," said Clara. "I was afraid that she would cause trouble with the Valentis next." The room was silent again for several moments while everyone processed the scene they had just witnessed.

"Well I don't know about the rest of you," said John Smith. "But I'm starved. Do you think we could go in for dinner now?"

"Let us go in to dinner," Mary said as calmly as she could. Even after that terrible confrontation, they felt as if a weight had lifted off the evening and they headed into the dining room.

William walked alongside Mary and gently squeezed her hand. "Remind me to never get on your bad side," he whispered with a smile.

CHAPTER 18

The next day at Davenport House was sunny and bright. Phillip and William were both invited to have lunch at the house. Everyone including Mrs. Price and the Valenti children were seated at the dining table. Everyone, that is, except for Mrs. Davenport.

"Mrs. Price, I am glad to see you at our table today," said Mary. "I hope that you will dine with us every day."

"I have come today at my daughter's request for a special occasion. But now that I have tasted the food, you may be assured of my return," Mrs. Price said, and everyone at the table laughed.

"I am happy to hear that we will see you more, but what is this special occasion?" asked Mary.

"Tell them, Miss Clara," said Gabriella impatiently.

Clara smiled when she realized that all eyes in the room were on her. "I do have something to tell, or rather to announce. Phillip and I are going to be married."

"What?" shrieked Mary. "Oh! My dear sister is going to be married!" She stood up from her seat and went to put her arms around Clara. Phillip was smiling brightly, and even Mrs. Price seemed cheerful to hear the news.

Ethan and Abigail looked at each other intently across the dining table. They had decided to delay the announcement of their own happy news so that Clara's engagement would get the attention that it deserved.

"Congratulations to you both," said William sincerely, all the while looking at Mary. Her cheeks were rosy with excitement and this was the most he had seen her smile.

After lunch, William could not wait to ask Mary a question. "Has your mother left for good?"

"She ordered for her belongings to be moved this morning before anyone else was awake. She will be living in a cottage that she inherited from Father," Mary said with a smile.

"And you have your house back," said William cheerfully. They walked to the front of the house where the others were gathered to admire William's car.

"Any chance you would permit me to take Clara and the children for a spin?" asked Phillip eagerly. "I drove sometimes for the boss in Pittsburgh."

"Be my guest," answered William happily.

"Oh, it is beautiful! This is my first time in an automobile!" Clara cried excitedly. The children climbed happily into the backseat. The Valentis drove off leaving William and Mary, Ethan and Abigail quietly standing in front of the house.

"Abigail," William finally said to break the silence. "Would you please show me the gardens again? They must be alive with color now."

"Certainly, William," smiled Abigail, hiding her surprise that he would not want to stay with Mary. Ethan looked at Abigail and nodded toward Mary, then Abigail smiled back at him and nodded. She then turned to William. "Let us take the longer path around the house."

As soon as William and Abigail had walked away, Mary demanded playfully, "What are these secret looks you and Abigail have been exchanging? You could not keep your eyes off each other all through lunch. Have you finally asked her?"

Ethan smiled. "I have."

"And she accepted?"

Ethan smiled again and nodded.

"Ethan, how wonderful! Oh no, this isn't wonderful! All of my friends are engaged, and I will be the old maid!" Mary groaned.

"Not a chance of that," laughed Ethan.

Abigail and William walked together in the gardens. William was correct that the trees and flowers were alive with color and seemed to be on parade in the shining sun. "There is something I have been wanting to ask you, Abigail," William began hesitantly.

"If you are asking for my hand, then you are too late. I have already accepted another," Abigail said with a smile.

"Oh! Truly? Um, no, I'm sorry. It was not that!" he stammered, then laughed. "I wanted to ask about Mary. How much longer until her mourning days are complete?"

"I expect she will always be mourning for her father, but I think you are only asking about her family's tradition. She has informed me that she will begin wearing colors in October. Why do you ask?" she questioned him, even though she knew the answer.

He was silent and sheepish for a moment, then began to laugh. "I am making a study of mourning traditions. Why else would I ask? Now, let us go back to see if Phillip and

Clara have returned with my car. The way that Phillip looked at it, I would not be so sure that he planned to return it to me at all!" William joked. But Phillip did return William's car, and Clara walked with the Valentis back to their farmhouse. Ethan and Abigail decided to ride the horses over the fields before dinner. William and Mary stood alone in front of the house just before William was preparing to leave.

"I am happy for your friends—all planning their weddings now," he said to Mary. "I think that I may be envious."

"You could plan a wedding yourself, if you wished," remarked Mary.

"Oh, I would like to very much," he said with a cheerful laugh. Then he seemed to suddenly become shy. "Mary, I wonder if perhaps we can continue this conversation sometime in the autumn."

"Well then, I cannot wait to see the leaves start to turn," Mary replied with a smile.

William smiled too. "I suppose I have to say goodbye now," he stalled.

"William," said Mary.

"Yes?" he answered hopefully.

"Do you think you will ever send us a bill?" she asked.

William laughed. "I will add it to my list of things to do when I reopen the clinic. Would that make you happy?"

"What would truly make me happy is for you to kiss me goodbye again. Only this time, I would not have to worry that it means it is the last time I will ever see you."

William smiled as he stepped closer to Mary and took her hand in his. "Then you will be seeing me often. If I may kiss you again now, I do not know how I could manage to keep away."

...excerpt from Book 3...

DAVENPORT HOUSE

A Mother's Love

MARIE SILK

John Smith sighed heavily. "Now I have told you every-thing, Son. There is something more I must show you." He kneeled to the floor in front of Maryanne's hope chest and lifted the heavy wooden lid. He carefully moved the items around inside, then reached to the very bottom. "Your ma wrote me a letter on that day. She said I should hear what it says someday after you were grown. I have been scared all these years of what it might tell me. I watched her cry as she wrote it. I already know she blames me for not bring-ing the doctor quick enough. I know everything was my fault. I kept her last words tucked away, figuring they must be real bad if she couldn't just tell me herself. She knew that I couldn't read or write. Maybe she thought I would learn someday." He solemnly handed Ethan a folded paper with writing on both sides.

"You want me to read it to you now, Pa?" Ethan asked uncertainly. He had not seen his father this distressed before, and he certainly did not want to make it worse.

John Smith took a deep breath and lowered himself onto the chair across from Ethan. "I think it's time I hear what she says. That night the old stable caught fire, I was afraid her words to me would get lost forever. Perhaps I should not have waited this long. Just read it to me and keep reading, no matter how bad it gets. I deserve what she says about me."

Ethan unfolded the letter and began to skim the page. He suddenly felt the hair on his neck standing up and chills running down his back and arms. Ethan abruptly turned the letter to see the other side. The color drained from his face as he continued to read in silence. He felt as though time had stopped, and he could not be sure if he was even breathing.

"What is it?" his father pleaded in an anguished voice. "I knew it must be bad! I knew I never deserved her love!"

Ethan did not hear anything his father said. The words on the page blurred together in front of his eyes. He was in another time and another place, in a world where their lives could never be the same. He finally snapped out of it to the cries of his father, who was now weeping uncontrollably as he stood up to leave the room. "Pa, wait!" Ethan told him quickly. "Ma never blamed you—it was never your fault! She didn't want you to feel bad for any of it!"

John Smith clutched his chest and held onto the back of

a chair before he crumpled to the floor. "Why did you not just tell me, Son?" he cried in agony. "I was ready to die!"

Ethan could feel his heart pounding once more. "Pa, this letter—it's not what you think it is. It's not what you think at all."

About the Author

Marie Silk has enjoyed writing stories and plays since her childhood years. She lives with her family in the United States and frequently travels the globe to learn more about the world and the people in it. Marie is inspired by history and the feats of humanity from ancient civilization to present day. The Davenport House historical fiction saga is her first published series.

Emails may be sent to mariesilkpublishing@gmail.com.

Made in the USA
Lexington, KY
24 June 2019